KATY METZ

Jul!

For my parents, Peggy and Ken.
Yay!

Jul: (yool)
Archaic term for Christmas;
see also *ġéol, jól, yule*

Contents

1

It Begins

The room was empty. Moonlight streamed in through the large arched windows and illuminated the brick walls adorned with unlit torches. There was an iron chandelier hanging from the ceiling, a dead fireplace on one wall, and a wood-paneled door on the opposite wall.

The door flew open and in floated a white ethereal humanoid with a flame-like head. The chandelier lit up, and the fireplace and torches roared to life, bathing the room in a sinister fiery glow.

It was the Ghost of Christmas Past.

As he moved to the center of the room, he was followed by his cohorts, the Ghosts of Christmas Present and Yet to Come.

The Ghost of Christmas Present was a very tall, broad human who wore a long green robe trimmed in white fur and a crown of holly on his head. He had long, curly chestnut hair with a beard to match. The Ghost of Christmas Yet to Come wore a black hooded robe that exposed only the skeletal remains of his hands. He seemed to glide on air, as did the Ghost of Christmas Past.

The Ghosts of Christmas were followed into the room by a demon covered in brown fur and wearing a green hooded cape trimmed in grey fur. Krampus, the shadow of St. Nicholas, carried a bag, chain and flail. After Krampus came an enormous black cat with a candle on his head. He wore a red collar with a sprig of holly and festive bell under his chin and arched his back on the side of the doorframe as he entered the room. It was Jólakötturinn, the Christmas cat.

"Mew," he greeted the others. Krampus chucked him under the chin, and he began to purr loudly.

"Why has he called us here?" Present asked.

"*Ich weiss nicht*," Krampus said.

Present looked to Past. "What did he say?"

"I don't know."

"I really wish he spoke English," Present said.

"Mew."

Past rolled his eyes as a small plastic elf in a plush blue onesie with white trim and gold applique and a blue Santa-style hat marched into the room. Elf that Helps ™ was on a mission and everyone's attention turned to him. He stopped in front of the wall and

2

a projection screen unrolled behind him.

"Yet to Come, if you will."

Yet to Come slowly raised his arm and pointed at the screen. A collage of Christmas images appeared on it. They included a Nativity scene, a decorated tree, hot cocoa, candy canes and a family seated around a fireplace, presumably enjoying one another's company.

"Christmas." Elf whipped out a retractable pointer and hit the screen. "A time for kindness and generosity. A time for love and family and friendship. All of the things Christ himself embodied. The most wonderful time of the year. At least it used to be."

The collage disappeared in a graph, showing in red and green how appreciation for Christmas had gone down in recent years.

"Over time," he continued, "many people have lost interest in the true spirit of the holiday. Some are even starting to resent Christmas in general."

Everyone gasped.

"They are tired of what it has come to represent. Consumerism, greed. Another stress-filled obligation. They think there is no more magic and compassion in the world."

The situation was even more dire than Elf let on. If they didn't get at least one person to believe in and personify the true spirit of Christmas again soon, all the spirits would start to vanish. He didn't want to alarm his companions, so he thought it was best to keep that part a secret for the time being. He just had to get them to do the job. If they succeeded, it wouldn't matter anyway.

"So sad." Present shook his head.

"Mew."

"Yes, very sad. Which is the reason I called you here." A giant red box with a green question mark at the center appeared on the screen to replace the graph. Elf hit the box with his pointer. "In a moment, a database of all the people in the world will appear and one will be randomly selected. That will be our first project – to spread love and get that person to embrace the true spirit of Christmas again. Yet to Come, if you'll do the honors."

Yet to Come shook his outstretched finger and the question mark inside the box turned into pictures of people. The pictures flashed inside the box, eventually slowing down and landing on one of a woman, half-smiling. She was about 30 years old with long, dark hair and green eyes. She was average height, perhaps a little overweight but not obese. At the bottom of the picture, black text read:

Eliza Smith
  Whattown, Minnesota, U.S.A.

"Aah, Eliza Smith." Elf put his pointer back, pulled a list from his pocket, and began to scroll down it with his finger. "Here you are! First year on the naughty list but not completely lost. Only a little jaded. Perfect candidate for us to help celebrate Christmas the right way."

The screen began to retract and Yet to Come slowly lowered his arm. Elf rolled up the list and put it back in his pocket.

"Any ideas?"

"MEOW!"

"No. She just bought a new pair of socks. You can't eat her."

"Mew." Jólakötturinn never got to eat anyone anymore.

"Ich könnte sie in die Hölle ziehen."

"Dragging people to Hell is not the answer to everything, Krampus." Past rolled his eyes as Krampus shrugged and began teasing Jólakötturinn with his flail.

"Yes. Too extreme in this case," Elf said.

"I could show her how her family and friends are celebrating this year," Present suggested.

"She won't care. Besides, it's been done."

"Maybe if I helped her remember how Christmas used to be." Past brightened at the opportunity to get out and do what he did best.

"Yes, but you can both only be on Earth for a

limited amount of time and it might take longer than that. We need something more. Something unique. Something…"

Yet to Come pointed at the floor and carved a tombstone with Eliza Smith inside.

"Why do *you* want to kill her?" The drawing disappeared as Elf swiped the air above it and turned to Krampus, who was still playing with Jólakötturinn. "Are you two paying any attention?"

He stormed over, grabbed the flail out of Krampus' hand and threw it out a window.

Ever the predator, the festive feline sailed out after it.

They all watched and stood in silence as they heard a clink followed by a louder splat.

"Well, that was unfortunate." Elf turned back to the other Christmas spirits. "Now, an idea that doesn't kill Eliza." He looked at Krampus.

"Ich bringe sie in die Hölle." Krampus threw the side of his cape in the air, turned, and disappeared. Past's eyes widened in horror while Elf and the other Ghosts of Christmas stared in shock at where Krampus had been standing.

"Where's he going?" Present whispered to Past.

"He's going to find Eliza and bring her to Hell." Past was staring, stunned, at the empty spot.

"Well, we should stop him."

Past turned slowly and looked at Present with a

raised eyebrow. The word *Yes* was etched into the wall where Yet to Come pointed.

"His obsession with Hell is just…" Elf made a fist and began pacing. "I don't even know why I invite him anymore."

"Too late now." Present always was the helpful one.

"How are we going to stop him? He'll find her sooner or later and she'll be dead if we don't do something."

As if on cue, Krampus appeared in the same spot he had been standing minutes before. He had a woman thrown over his shoulder. Her face was covered by a curtain of long, dark hair. Yet to Come etched *Oh, no* into the wall.

"He got her." Present was dumbfounded.

"That was quick," Elf said.

"Put me down!" The woman kicked and punched Krampus as much as she was able.

"*Die Hölle würde sie nicht nehmen.*"

"So you brought her here?" Elf was surprised. They'd never had a human visitor before.

Past floated behind Krampus and moved the hair to get a look into the woman's eyes. "Of course they wouldn't take her in Hell. That's not Eliza."

"Eliza?" The woman stopped struggling.

"*Scheisse.*" Krampus dropped her on her feet. She brushed herself off.

7

"What is going on?" she demanded, looking at each of the spirits.

"This must be Eliza's cousin Jackie. On the nice list, of course. I've been told they look a lot alike." Elf turned from the Ghosts of Christmas as Yet to Come etched *Hi* on a brick in Jackie's line of vision. "And you, Jackie, are in the headquarters of the Christmas spirits."

"Christmas spirit headquarters. Okay." Jackie nodded and pinched herself while whispering mantras to wake up.

"Ich werde jetzt Eliza bekommen."

"No, you're not going to get her now." Past grabbed Krampus' cape just as he lifted it to disappear into oblivion again. Krampus huffed and crossed his arms over his chest.

"Krampus seems to have made a mistake. He was searching for your cousin, Eliza," Elf told Jackie.

"Uh-huh." Jackie wasn't buying it.

"Really. She's on the naughty list. He wanted to bring her to Hell, but…got you instead."

Krampus shrugged. What can you do? Accidents happen.

"Oh. Then I can wake up now or something?"

"Uh…well…"

"Well, what? This is a dream, isn't it?"

"Not exactly." Elf said, shifting his weight from side to side.

8

"Uh-huh." Jackie tapped her foot. "I just want to go home. Do I click my heels together three times or what?"

"Well...um...it's not that easy. See, you're...uh...well...actually...you're..."

Yet to Come carved a tombstone with *Jackie Miller* written on it. Jackie's eyes widened in horror.

"I'M DEAD?!"

"Yes." Elf looked meekly at Jackie.

"Oh my God. OH MY GOD!" Jackie began hyperventilating.

"Don't worry..."

"Don't worry!? I'M DEAD!"

Elf sighed. "Yes, when Krampus gets a hold of someone their soul leaves their body. That's true...but we still have your soul."

"Oh." Jackie looked anxiously at Elf. "So you can put me back in my body?"

"No."

"And I'm supposed to stop worrying?!"

Past floated up to Jackie and put his hand on her shoulder. Her breathing slowed and her body slackened a little. Her eyes glazed over and a gimpy smile filled her face.

Elf continued explaining the situation. "Your soul needs to go into a different body. Living or unborn, your choice. But it would be too much of a shock for others if your body was resurrected."

9

"It happened once and they started a religion," Past said.

"*Living* body?" Jackie was confused. Didn't every living being already have a soul?

"Yes. Think of it as a soul transplant for a broken soul," Elf said.

"Oh." Jackie considered this for a second. "What do you think it's like to be a cat?"

Past looked at her with a raised eyebrow and removed his hand from her shoulder. She seemed calm enough. That's when Elf got an idea. He knew exactly how to motivate the rest of the spirits to help Eliza without telling them they'd disappear if they didn't.

"Krampus, you want to take Eliza to Hell, right?"

"*Ja!*" Krampus lifted the edge of his cape and Past grabbed it again, his gaze never leaving Elf.

"We'll let you."

"What?!" Past, Present, and Jackie gasped in unison. Yet to Come carved out an Edvard Munch painting on the wall.

"Yes. We're going to let Krampus take Eliza to Hell. *If* she doesn't remember the true spirit of Christmas by Christmas Eve."

"And how are we going to make her remember the true spirit of Christmas?" Present asked. "You haven't liked any of our ideas."

"Maybe you should go to her yourself," Past

suggested to Elf. Yet to Come wrote *Yes* on another brick.

"No, she doesn't own one of my portals. I can't just show up."

As Elf pondered, the large wooden door creaked open. In the frame stood Julbok, a white goat with red and white striped horns that looked exactly like candy canes.

Elf's mouth twisted into a grin. "But he can."

"Meh."

2

Wednesday, December 16th

The minister droned on about ashes to ashes. I was sitting in the church staring at a large crucifix hanging above the altar. It was draped with gold silky looking fabric and flanked by a white angel on each side. To the right of the altar were four unlit candles, three purple and one pink, sitting uncontained in a wreath of evergreen. In front of the altar were poinsettias and a closed casket with a sprig of holly on top. Even at a funeral, I couldn't escape Christmas.

Something about Christmas makes me uncomfortable. Maybe it's Santa. "He sees you when you're sleeping, he knows when you're awake." Forces reindeer to pull him around in a sleigh, enslaves elves, runs a sweatshop. No wonder Santa is an anagram for Satan.

As a child, all year-round, I was told, "Don't talk

to strangers!" Then come Christmas, it was, "Go sit on this random man's lap and tell him what you want." Apparently only strangers wearing red with white beards were okay.

Maybe it's the fact that you can't find a parking spot anywhere and every store is magically packed with people.

Maybe it's all the songs and carols with their cringey lyrics that don't make any sense.

Maybe it's all the family time and forced togetherness. Not that I hate my family, but they prefer my brother and cousins to me, so I keep my distance. They get together often since we're all in the same general area and usually I avoid that if I can come up with an excuse. But I feel obligated to join them for special events like holidays and funerals.

Maybe it's all the peppermint.

It doesn't matter why, really. I just can't get into Christmas. Not anymore, anyway. The older I get, the more terrible it becomes. The endless parties, all the food you eat only because it's the holidays (much of it some "limited edition" flavor that will come back next year), decorating your house, and for what? One day. All the buildup and by the time Christmas actually rolls around, people are completely burned out.

And don't get me started on gift giving. What's the point? I'd rather save the money for things I want for myself. Even though Christmas throws up everywhere (earlier and earlier each year, it seems), I've always done my best to acknowledge it as little as possible. Not always the easiest task, but it was now less than 10 days away and I just had to get through it.

One and a half weeks. It really doesn't sound so bad when you put it that way, and it'll go fast. I hope.

I focused on the sunlight streaming in through the stained-glass windows. It was the middle of December, in Minnesota, and a perfect 65 degrees outside. That gave me something positive to think about and it made me happy.

"Eliza!" my mom whispered sharply. I quickly dropped the smile I didn't realize I was wearing.

"What?"

"Stand up. They're about to take your cousin's body out." She looked back toward the altar. As I scanned the church, I noticed that everyone was already standing. Sheepishly, I stood, cleared my throat, and straightened my skirt. No one would notice, right?

"And whenever a bell rings, an angel will get its wings," the minister somberly concluded while cheerful sleigh bells rang from somewhere unknown.

They were really trying to incorporate Christmas,

weren't they? Did Jackie seriously like Christmas that much?

The pallbearers lifted the casket and walked slowly forward as my Aunt Karen and Uncle Frank followed my erstwhile cousin's body out of the church. Once the casket reached the doors, everyone began to filter out behind the bereaved parents. I stood on my toes to search for an exit route. Sandwiched in the middle of the pew, I wasn't going anywhere anytime soon. I concentrated on the music now filling the church to distract myself as I waited. A bagpipe version of "Silent Night"? Honestly.

Once I made it outside, I watched across the parking lot as the hearse doors closed behind the casket. My parents went to greet some relative or other while Karen and Frank talked with the minister next to hearse. The minister held Karen's hand while Frank stood stoically to the side. I walked up to them as the minister gave Karen a hug and left to get into a car.

"I'm so sorry about Jackie." I said as I reached the hearse.

"Thanks, Eliza," Frank said with barely a glance. Hands buried in the pockets of his suit pants, he turned away to look at the church and the sun glinted off his balding head. The greying hair that formed his developing tonsure was dark once.

"Oh, come here." Tears began to well in Karen's small blue eyes. I caught of whiff of citrus from her short, curly rust-blonde hair. "I'm so happy you made it today. It would mean so much to Jackie to know you're here." Her thick Minnesota accent was even more pronounced when she was sad, I noticed.

"Yeah…" I backed out of the tight embrace.

I was never particularly close to Jackie. We were the same age, down to the month, except I was born earlier in October, and we had been in school together. In fact, we were often mistaken for twins but couldn't be more opposite, and a relationship just never developed. Honestly, I probably wouldn't have known her at all if we weren't related. She'd been much closer to my younger brother Adam. But he was off in Kenya in the Peace Corps, so of course I had to represent even though they would have preferred him to me. Mom wouldn't let me out of it. Story of my life.

"You being here…it's just like she's here, too." Karen dabbed her eyes with her black chiffon shawl and looked at me wistfully.

"Heh." I wasn't sure what to say. I fully recognize that Jackie and I looked alike, but hearing that at her funeral and from her mother, no less…why did I come over here again? "So, I'll see you at the cemetery then."

Frank nodded silently once, and Karen bobbed

16

her head, beginning to sob.

I looked toward the church and waved at my parents, then turned back to Karen and Frank.

"See you there." I said awkwardly as I walked to my car.

The drive to the cemetery took me through a neighborhood I'd seen a few times, but now it really struck me how uncheerful all the Christmas decorations looked without snow. An inflatable snowman in one yard looked particularly out of place in the sunshine. The wreaths, tinsel snowflakes and tinsel bells on the streetlights when I turned onto the main street and entered the town were even more laughable.

My entire family and I lived in a town about 40 minutes south of Minneapolis called Whattown. With a population of about 15,000, it's not small but not exactly huge, either. It's growing every day, though, and with each passing year something closes while two new things spring up in its place. I both love and hate it.

I want to get some distance from my family and say I lived somewhere other than my hometown for at least a little while, but it is a nice and supposedly up-and-coming area. There's a movie theatre, recently updated bowling alley, several strip malls, and plenty of bars and restaurants to entertain the ever growing populous. The centerpiece of the town, however, was the park. You'd almost believe it was summer based on the weather and crowd gathered there this afternoon.

In the park stands a giant straw yule goat. It's something the local Scandinavian society puts up every year in December, and people love it. Case in point; they were gathered around it even in the middle of a weekday afternoon. I had never paid too much attention to it until that moment. It was really very intricate – amazing details. It must have taken days to shape the straw and what I imagined was an army of volunteers. I began to wonder how much straw was used and where it all came from. Most of the farms in the immediate area had been taken over for new infrastructure, so they probably brought it in from somewhere farther south. Maybe Iowa? Yards of red cloth were wrapped around the goat body to add color to the straw, and it looked like the cloth might have even had some kind of pattern on it that became more pronounced the longer I stared.

I was now wondering how long it might have taken to make when a car horn snapped me back to reality. I didn't even realize I had stopped. The light was yellow and turned red as I passed through the intersection. Oops!

I soon arrived at the cemetery and Jackie's casket was suspended over a rectangular pit. Someone had added one of those creepy Elf That Helps toys to the sprig of holly. Rest in peace, indeed. I rolled my eyes and took a seat in a folding chair that had been arranged around the burial site. My parents joined me as the last few funeral goers took their seats and the final part of the funeral began.

After a couple minutes with the sun beating down and the slight breeze, it hit me all at once how exhausted I really was. I nearly dozed off a few times while the minister performed the burial rites.

"That God may accept sister Jackie into His kingdom, let us..." He looked at the casket and cleared his throat. "Let us pray."

We all stood and joined hands. The congregation began chanting the Lord's Prayer.

"Our Father, who art in Heaven..."

It was so rhythmic and the fact that everybody knew the words made it feel like we were performing some kind of secret ritual. At "thy kingdom come", I caught the minister again glancing at the casket and saw the lid move subtly. My eyes widened but I continued speaking the words.

Thy will be done...

I scanned the rest of the crowd. Nobody else seemed to notice the casket lid moving. Maybe the minister was just looking at the Elf toy and I was seeing things. I blinked to refocus and continued the prayer.

Give us this day our daily bread...

At "lead us not into temptation", the minister let out a shriek and jumped back two feet as the casket lid opened completely and Jackie's hand reached out to grab the side of the casket.

Slowly, she climbed out, looking like one of those Japanese ghost girls with the long dark hair hiding their faces. Her white dress with leopard print trim was a little frayed along the edges and her skin was an ashen grey.

By now, the minister was halfway to his car. The rest us jumped out of our seats screaming and everyone began to scatter, knocking over chairs and leaving light jackets and purses in their wake. In my panic, I just stood there, trying to remember where I parked as Jackie staggered closer. She lifted her head, directed her gaze to mine, and suddenly, like a horror movie killer, she was standing next to me. She never lost eye contact.

I shuddered.

"Hi, Eliza."

I took a step backward. "H-hey, Jackie."

"Nice of you to come to my funeral."

"Wouldn't miss it."

"Right. You know, they say two people can never go to each other's funerals? If it were possible, I'd go to yours, too."

"Uh-huh." I took another step backward and

20

bumped into a chair. I turned to watch the chair tip over.

"I would. And I wouldn't be thinking about how I didn't want to be there. Especially if I was the reason there was a funeral in the first place."

"What?" I'm pretty damn sure I had nothing to do with Jackie's death. Come to think of it, I didn't even know how she died.

"He thought I was you."

"Who?"

"You don't ever want to find out. It was terrible."

"Oh." My heart began to pound. I looked to the ground where a large spider crawled across Jackie's foot and went up her leg, disappearing under her dress. She didn't seem to notice. I gulped. "So, uh…how…how exactly did you die?"

"He thought I was you."

"Yeah, you said, but I don't understand." I started to worry my shirt hem.

"You'll understand soon enough. Especially if you don't change your attitude."

"My attitude?"

"Yes."

"I don't have –"

"Oh, come on. You're jaded and cynical. You visit your family but you never enjoy it."

"Well, I…" I backed up to stand behind a chair and clutched the top of it. Where did I put my car keys?

Out of habit, I patted my hips to search even though my skirt didn't have pockets.

"You're selfish, too."

"Selfish?"

"When was the last time you did something for someone else?"

"I don't remember, but I –"

"Exactly. That's why you're on the naughty list." Jackie appeared right next to me. Startled, I gasped and almost threw the chair to the ground.

"What?" Then I realized something. "Wait. How do I know I'm not dreaming right now? You're probably not even real." I didn't have anything to worry about. I pinched myself on the arm to make sure.

Nothing.

Crap.

Jackie closed her eyes and a wind blew up from beneath her, making the skirt of her dress balloon and her long dark hair stand on end, like thin spikes, framing her face. When her eyes opened, they had become an ethereal laser-blue color.

"They're real, Eliza, and they're trying to save you from him."

"Who's real?" My heart was still racing, and I began to pant. Save me? From who? Santa? What kind of danger was I in, exactly? The wind stopped and Jackie was a normal corpse again.

"This will be you if you're not careful." She gestured to herself, presumably to highlight her sunken eyes, ashen skin, and general corpse-ness.

"How can I be careful if I don't know what you're talking about?"

"You'll see. His mistake means you're getting a second chance. Don't blow it."

She shoved me violently and I jerked awake with a snort. In front of me, the minister was completing the burial rites and the still closed casket was being lowered into the ground. Mom looked at me disapprovingly, and I grinned guiltily.

3

Meanwhile

"**G**ood. Jackie warned her." Elf removed goggles with dark lenses from his eyes and pocketed them. "I'm glad we could persuade her to help after what happened last week."

He was standing next to Julbok by the fireplace while the Ghosts of Christmas were seated at a table with Krampus. They each held cards in their hands and the rest of the deck was in a stack on the table next to Yet to Come.

"She seemed happy with our bargain. I just hope we can make it reality." Past said, drawing a new card.

"It should be easy enough."

Present flipped through his cards thoughtfully and pointed to the deck. "Hit me."

Yet to Come dealt Present a new card. Present added it to those already in his hand, only to toss them all onto the table seconds later.

"Dang it, 22."

Krampus lay a card on top of one of Present's and was left with one remaining in his hand.

"*Ein.*"

"Why are you saying one? I thought we were playing Texas Hold'em," Past said, fanning his cards out.

Yet to Come drew a new card and lay four queens on the table, confident that would win whatever game they were playing.

Suddenly, Jackie materialized in a cloud of glittering dust. She brushed some of the sparkle from her shoulder and walked over to Elf and Julbok.

"There."

"Well done."

"So, can we do it now?"

"Soon. First we need to get Julbok to Earth."

"Meh," the goat bleated.

"*Ich werde jetzt Eliza bekommen.*" Krampus stood, threw his card on the table, and made to grab his cape.

Past was the first to grab the cape and pulled Krampus down again. "You're not going anywhere."

"Harrumph." Krampus pursed his lips and crossed his arms.

"We need a portal for Julbok," Elf said. He tapped his finger on his lips for a few seconds and lifted it when he had the solution. "Past?"

Past lit up even brighter and set his cards on the table.

"Leave it to me." He left in a flash and landed in Whattown Park next to the straw yule goat.

There was a sizable crowd, but Past was invisible unless he wanted to be seen. He observed that even though the adults were outwardly happy to be there, they radiated stress and anxiety. That could easily be fixed, and since he was already there, he began tapping people on the shoulder as he made a quick lap around the yule goat.

Once tapped, a mother remembered her now college-aged child's first Christmas. A man in his 80s remembered taking wooden sleds with metal runners to the top of snow-covered hills and riding down with his friends. A woman in her 40s remembered baking cookies with her grandmother. They each smiled warm, genuine smiles and visibly relaxed. As Past completed his lap, the smiles spread. That accomplished, he floated up to the straw goat and touched it, admired it. Past appreciated folk art.

With a deep breath, he crouched and drifted under the yule goat. With a twirl of his head, the goat ignited. Past watched for a moment as the crowd began to gasp and scream when they noticed the growing flames. In another brilliant flash, Past returned to headquarters, where Elf and the others were waiting.

"It's done."

Elf turned toward the fireplace and watched as glowing embers started to appear. He looked at Julbok.

"It's time."

Julbok stepped into the fireplace and the flames began to grow higher. Past and Present waved to Julbok and Yet to Come gave a one finger salute. Krampus had gone to the corner to mourn the loss of Jólakötturinn and his chance to get Eliza.

"Good luck," Elf called into the fireplace as the flames engulfed Julbok and sucked him into the ether.

4

Wednesday, December 16th
(continued)

Now that the service had ended, there was one hurdle left to jump over before I could go home. I had to join my family at Aunt Karen and Uncle Frank's house for a post funeral lunch. Mom insisted I stay for the whole day so I could get pictures to send to Adam. Go figure.

The food had better be worth it.

Karen and Frank's house looked like it was straight out of a Christmas movie. Not a corner went unadorned in red, green, gold, or silver. Nary a shelf was saved from the presence of a gilded nativity scene or Santa statue. A tree (fully decorated, of course) stood prominently in a bay window. Even though sunlight flooded in, the tree lights were glowing dimly.

Choking down eggnog my cousin Tim distributed, I wandered aimlessly. Smiling superficially at the other guests, answering the same questions over and over, and sitting awkwardly at the kitchen table, using my teeth to decapitate the tiny gingerbread men that had been set out. As I ate each gingerbread man I beheaded, my thoughts wandered to how such a delicious spicy flavor got to be associated with Christmas.

That's when Tim's wife Rachel and their baby Avery joined me at the table. She popped a whole gingerbread man into her mouth while Avery pulled her mom's light brown hair.

"Hey!" Rachel adjusted Avery on her lap as she sat in the vacant chair next to me.

"Hi."

"How are you?"

"I'm all right."

"Good. So, how is Adam doing in Africa?" Rachel perked up and skillfully ignored Avery's tugging at her shirt.

"Fine, I guess." I turned my phone in my hand and remembered I was supposed to be taking pictures. "Hey, can we get a picture to send him?"

I angled my phone to get the three of us, already knowing what the answer would be.

"Absolutely. Avery, look at the camera."

Rachel pointed and Avery cooed at the sight of

herself on the screen. I pressed the button to take a picture and Avery reached for it, but Rachel stood and positioned the baby on her hip.

"No, that's not for you. We need to take care of this situation." Rachel pinched her nose shut to indicate Avery had a full diaper. "Great to see you, Eliza."

She gave me a partial wave as they walked off toward the bathroom.

"Yeah."

I opened the email app on my phone and started a new email addressed to Adam. Without any message or subject line, I attached the image and sent it off. Mission accomplished.

* * *

Lunch was ham, mashed potatoes and green beans. When it was served at long last, I sat between my mom and Aunt Nancy and hastily shoveled food into my mouth. The sooner I finished, the sooner I could claim my candy cane (for dessert, naturally) and get out.

Mom looked over at me. "You must be hungry."

"Mmm–" *Something like that.*

"You know, the open house goes until 3. You don't have to rush," Mom returned to her own meal, making a show of eating slowly. Great. We still had three and a half more hours. Dad looked at me from across the table and raised his chin in the air to tell me to sit up straight. I rolled my eyes and corrected my posture.

Secretly, I hoped this would double as the annual family Christmas gathering. There were enough festive foods and decorations to make anyone forget there had been a funeral. Karen and Mom were even talking excitedly as they ate.

"I could make a nice Hot Dish," Mom said to Karen, who was just getting up to go to the kitchen.

You can't get more Minnesotan than Hot Dish. It's tater tots, a "cream of" soup (think cream of chicken or cream of mushroom), usually some cheese and whatever vegetables and meat you want all baked together. It's quick, easy, and definitely not a casserole, though I'm not sure exactly what the difference is. Not my favorite, but my family loves it, and someone makes it almost every time we get together. What were they planning now?

"That would be lovely." Karen said before she walked off, her shoulder length curly hair bouncing behind her.

"I'll bring a side dish," Frank said.

"That'd be great," Dad said.

"Make a Hot Dish for what, Mom?"

"Karen and Frank are coming over for lunch on Saturday with Steve, Nancy, and Tim and his family."

"Looking forward to it," Tim said, putting baby Avery into a highchair.

Karen and Frank, I can tolerate. They've always been cordial with me, and from time to time, it even seems sincere. Tim, Rachel and Avery are fine. I rarely see them because Rachel's schedule as a doctor is hectic, so I have no reason to dislike them. Steve is even okay in small doses. He'll talk to me but I feel like he's only doing it out of obligation. Nancy, however, is a different story. Whenever she talks to me, I feel so small and condescended to, even though she never says anything truly terrible. Her hair is also always swept into an updo and she's rail thin. That with her bulging blue eyes make her even look intimidating.

"It's too bad Nicole won't be there," Dad said, indicating my redheaded cousin who was in her sophomore year at college in Buffalo. She idolized Jackie when she was little, and they were basically sisters. I was not at all surprised to see her at the funeral, but it must have been a hell of an expensive flight last minute.

"Yeah." Nicole tucked her hair behind her ear and looked away from Dad.

"It'll be a nice chance to get together again just before Christmas." Karen set a bowl of fresh rolls in front of us before returning to her seat at the end of the table.

"*Before* Christmas?" I gasped. That's more than three times in less than two weeks.

"Yes, but don't worry. We'll still get together on Christmas, too," Mom said.

"Oh, good."

"You can join us Saturday, too, if you want, but you're probably busy." Mom took a sip of her water and Karen looked at me eagerly. Here comes the guilt, right on cue.

"Er, well, the thing is…"

"It's okay. We understand," Nancy said.

"Uh-huh." Phew.

"I wish Jackie could be there." Karen sniffled and grabbed the black shawl still draped over her shoulders, threatening to dab her eyes again.

"Yes, the first Christmas without her will be extra hard for you, I'm sure." Mom looked at me out of the corner of her eye.

"It will be different."

Karen and Mom were both staring at me now. Karen seemed both sad and hopeful at the same time. I bit my lip. Maybe I could just stop by for a few minutes?

"Well, I suppose I…"

"Great! We'll see you on Saturday," Mom said with a smile. Karen dropped her shawl and went back to her meal.

"But I can only –"

"No need to bring anything, dear. Just show up at 1." Mom sipped her water again and she turned away to end our conversation.

"Okay." I slumped in my chair and with a happy squeal, Avery threw a little piece of roll that landed on my lap. Nicole watched me and bounced a little as she stifled a laugh. I brushed off the crumb.

Nancy caught her daughter snickering and looked at her sternly.

"You'd be going, too, if you weren't going back to New York to finish your finals."

"Yes, Mom." Nicole took a bite of ham.

"So, Eliza," Nancy turned her attention to me, "Is Adam still having a good time in Kenya?"

"As far as I know." It had been about two weeks since I'd spoken to him, but he seemed happy, I guess.

"It's so wonderful what he's doing over there with the Peace Corps. He's always been so big hearted."

"Mh-mm." My brother, the golden child.

"And your mom says he found a girlfriend. That's fantastic."

"Yep."

"Are you still seeing…is it James?"

It was Jason. We dated for five years, but he turned out to be more other than significant. And no. We hadn't been together for almost two years. "No, why?"

"Oh, I'm so sorry to hear that," Karen said. "I always liked *Josh*." She looked at Nancy.

"Yeah." I sighed.

"Yes, too bad." Nancy gave me feigned pity and pretended to ponder for a second. "Say, I noticed the graphic designer at the office isn't wearing a ring and he can't be more than a couple years older than you." She took a sip of water. I gritted my teeth. Here we go.

"Heh. Well…"

"Mom, Eliza doesn't need that." Nicole set her glass down on the table. "*If* she decides to date, she can find someone for herself. Besides, rings can come off."

"Don't be rude, dear. I'm talking to your cousin."

"But I don't think she wants to talk about that right now. Do you, Eliza?" Nicole looked at me.

"Er, actually…"

"See? Can we drop it now?"

"I think it would be nice for Eliza to meet some new people," Mom said, joining the conversation. I swear she has a sixth sense and just knows when anyone mentions me dating.

"And if the graphic designer doesn't work out, the neighbor's have a son about your age in law school," Nancy said.

"Oh, a *lawyer*." Mom nodded encouragingly.

"Yeah, great." I twirled my fork on my plate and began jiggling my leg.

"Pass the potatoes?" Steve asked Dad. Dad grabbed the bowl of potatoes and passed it down.

"But who Eliza's dating is none of your business." Nicole slammed her hand down on the table. I dropped my fork and started worrying the hem of my shirt.

"Okay," Nancy opened her mouth to speak, but Nicole interrupted her.

"Besides, it doesn't matter if she's dating or not. It's pretty sexist to assume she wants a relationship."

Fiddling with the edge of my shirt knocked my napkin off my lap. It was right beside Nancy's foot. Crap!

"Can we stop talking about me like I'm not here?" I asked.

"See? Let's just drop it," Nicole said.

My eyes moved from Nancy to Nicole as I backed my chair out to make room to duck under the table. I bent over and almost had my napkin, but Frank, who was seated across from Nancy, moved his leg and brought it under his chair with his foot.

"You are really making this a big issue. Maybe I should help you find a date instead, hmm?" Nancy asked Nicole.

"Here we go. 'Give me more grandkids!'" I peeked up to see Nicole making air quotes with her fingers.

I bent back under the table. I just had to reach a little farther…

"Sorry you're not good enough, Avery." I saw Nicole's torso shift to face her niece.

Steve cleared his throat and I imagine he shook his head at Nicole. I could picture Nancy glaring at her as she spoke. "Do you really want to start this right now?"

"Ah-ha!" I snatched the napkin and came up to move my chair closer to the table. "Got it." I waved the napkin meekly to no one in particular and returned to my meal.

"Do *you*?" Nicole stood and pushed her chair in before walking away.

"So how about those Timberwolves?" Frank took a bite of green beans and looked around the table.

"I won tickets from a fundraiser at work, so I'm actually going to a game tomorrow," Tim said.

"That'll be nice." Karen smiled.

* * *

After all the family togetherness, I was physically and emotionally drained. I couldn't get home fast enough. I lived alone, and I was happy to be able to escape to solitude when I needed to.

I had a cozy one-level ranch house with three bedrooms and one and a half bathrooms. The living room even had a fireplace and there was a small dining area off the kitchen. There was no garage, but there was a driveway, so I didn't even have to park in the street. I also had a small patio in the backyard and a stoop for a porch outside the front door. I think the house was built in the 1960s? I'm renting it from a man my parents introduced me to who owns a couple other properties in town, and he maintains it pretty well so it's in fairly good condition considering the age.

Soon after I walked in the front door, I poured myself a glass of wine and sank into the couch in hopes of finding something mind-numbing on TV. What came on was a news reporter from a local TV station standing in front of the same straw yule goat I drove past earlier talking about arson.

The goat was on fire.

So, they got to it again this year.

The flames were almost a mile high and you could practically feel the heat through the screen. Who had managed to get close enough with all those witnesses this time? I didn't know whether to be appalled or impressed, honestly. You'd think the police would learn by now since someone tries to burn it down every year.

The backlighting darkened the reporter's face. It seemed the bigger the fire, the bigger the number of mesmerized by-standers. Some pointed in awe, some shook their heads in disbelief, and…was one holding a stick with a marshmallow at the end? The reporter continued to draw out the story as the goat fire raged on.

"The local police are still searching for information to help identify possible suspects. Until then, we can see the blazing yule before us. Back to you…"

I rolled my eyes as the anchors in the studio continued talking about the combusted caprine. I changed the channel only to find *A Christmas Carol*. Fantastic. I scoffed as I turned off the TV. I was ready to go eat dinner anyway.

5

Thursday, December 17th

At precisely 5:30 the next morning, my alarm went off. I slapped the snooze button and rolled over. I teach at Whattown Elementary and dreaded going to work this time of year. The kids were dreaming of sugar-plums and snow days instead of paying attention and forget about trying to get a hold of parents to address problems. They're caught up in holiday prep and don't really want to notice how their kids are doing in school. That's a problem to deal with in the New Year.

And don't even get me started on those teacher gifts. The last thing I want is another kitschy snowman that says *#1 Teacher*. I have an army of them in my desk drawer at school that I'm going to take to a thrift store at some point.

My alarm buzzed again. I pressed the Off button

and rolled out of bed. I stretched my arms and yawned as I pulled on a robe, proceeded to the bathroom and brushed my teeth before hopping in the shower. I relished the hot water as I lathered up. Once I ran out of things to wash, I stood under the steady stream and wondered for a couple minutes what would happen if I never got out. It was so warm, like a blanket. I pursed my lips as I turned off the water off and got ready to step out. Maybe next time I'll stay in there forever. Or until the hot water runs out...you know, whichever happens first.

I put my robe back on and started to dry my hair, which always feels like it takes forever but in reality is probably less than ten minutes. My hair is just a little below my shoulders, but it's pretty thick. When my hair was done, I padded back to the bedroom and walked to the dresser. Today I selected a pair of grey pants and a silky pale pink blouse. I dressed and chose a necklace with an opal pendant. I wish I had earrings to match, but the necklace is still pretty on its own. Once I was finished, I went to the kitchen to pour myself a bowl of cereal. I mindlessly played on my phone while I ate, scrolling through social media and checking the news. Sometimes we talked about current events in class and it was always a good idea to be ahead of the game so I could prepare a kid-friendly way to explain anything major that may have happened.

After I finished eating, I dropped the dishes in the sink and got ready to head out the door.

School starts at 8 and I walked into the building around 7:15 to find Kylie (Ms. Olson to her students) in my classroom. Kylie also taught second grade in the classroom next to mine. This morning, she was dressed in what could be called an ugly sweater with a reindeer, black felt skirt and black suede boots trimmed in faux fur at the top and opening around the laces. With her blonde hair braided down her back and her blue eyes, you couldn't possibly look any more stereotypically Scandinavian than she did that day.

"Morning!" she practically sang.

"Hi, Kylie." I walked to my desk to put my bag down and take off the light jacket I put on to ward off the slight chill in the morning air. "You look festive."

"I tried. It's really hard with all those rules David gave us."

David Smith is the school district superintendent. At the end of November, he held a district wide faculty meeting to tell us that we were supposed to avoid anything that could in any way, shape, or form be associated specifically with Christmas while we were on the clock and working with students. Personally, I found it reasonable. It was just like any other month of the year then and offered some reprieve from the outside world. Others planned subtle ways to rebel. I even heard a rumor that a first grade teacher was going to teach patterns with red and white stripes in an upside-down J shape.

Kylie apparently picked this outfit.

"That sweater is…"

"It's Nordic. I'm celebrating my Scandinavian heritage." She gave a little twirl.

"Is that what you call it?" I smirked.

Kylie rolled her eyes. "Anyway, I brought you coffee." She pointed at a cup next to the computer on my desk. "I wanted to say I'm sorry about Jackie."

"Thanks."

"Anytime."

I grabbed the cup and took a sip. Black. Perfect. "Hey, how's your cat doing?"

"Sia? She's a little better, I guess. She's started drinking again but now she can't get enough water and started peeing everywhere."

"Oh, no." I sat down and turned on my computer.

"Yeah, I think she may just be over-stimulated. She loves the tree. That with drinking too much…but I'm going to take her to the vet tonight just to be sure."

"Good luck."

"Thanks." Her previously bright expression had dimmed a little. "Well, I'd better get going to finish grading those last few quizzes."

"Okay. Thanks again for the coffee." I raised my cup as she went to her classroom. I turned my attention to the computer and had barely begun checking emails when my first student arrived. It was Tommy Carter and he ran straight up to my desk with a wide grin, his wavy brown hair bouncing and he made eye contact with me the whole way.

"Hi, Tommy. What can I do for you?"

"This is for you, Miss Smith." He produced a carved wooden snowman with a sled on one side that said *#1 Teacher* and put it on my desk.

"Thanks." I waited until his back was turned and put the snowman into the drawer with the others while he went to sit down.

Aiden James came in next, deep in conversation with Aubrey Moskowitz and Olivia Larson.

"You mean you only get presents on one day *and* you have to wait until the 25th?" Aubrey asked the others.

"Yeah, you get presents before Christmas?" Aiden asked.

"For eight days!" Aubrey said as she reached into her backpack to pull out a doll that probably wouldn't look so perfect by next week. "I got this last night."

"She's pretty," Olivia said.

"I wish I got presents for eight days," Aiden said.

He, Aubrey and Olivia all sat in their seats. I stood as the final bell rang and the last couple stragglers sat down.

At Whattown Elementary, I taught every subject and was responsible for planning my own class schedule. As long as I stuck to the prescribed curriculum, it didn't matter when during the day we covered the material. This morning, I decided we were going to start with science. We were going through the different ecosystems on Earth, beginning with the ocean. We'd finished that about two weeks ago and had moved on to the jungle unit, which ended with animals yesterday when my sub showed a video about monkeys, sloths and parrots.

I went to the white board and wrote *The Desert* in blue marker. I turned from the board and saw Isaac Johnson had raised his hand.

"Isaac?"

"What flavor is it?"

"What?"

"The dessert?"

"You mean the *desert*?"

"Yeah, what flavor is it?" He was completely serious.

"It doesn't have –"

"Is it like ice cream?" Olivia Larson asked, throwing her hand in the air.

"Not exactly."

"Cake?"

"No…"

"Then what flavor is it?" Isaac persisted. He pushed his glasses farther up onto his nose as he stared at me through the lenses.

"Sand, I guess?"

"Huh." Isaac cocked his head and seemed satisfied. A couple other students nodded, as if to say *Oh, of course. Sand.*

"Okay. Everyone, open your science books to page 35."

They each took their (only slightly) outdated science books and flipped through to the appropriate page while I found it in my teacher's edition. There were pictures of desert animals and plants, including cacti, and a definition of the word desert.

"So, most of the time when you think of a desert, you think of sand and heat. But really, a desert can be any place where there's little or no precipitation. Like Antarctica." I looked up from the book and Samantha Anthony had raised her hand. "Yes, Samantha?"

"My mom has a toy that looks like a cactus!"

I paused and stared at her. Then looked back at the page in front of me. The cacti had no branches.

Oh boy. I sighed. It was going to be one of those days.

***

Later that night, I woke up at the end of a dream and sat up in bed to look at the clock on the nightstand. It was 2:30 a.m. I lay back down and closed my eyes in an attempt to get back to sleep. About 20 minutes later I was roused again; this time by a persistent tapping coming from the front door. Someone at the door at 3 a.m. means it's either really important or I'm going to die. Best go find out.

My mind still foggy with sleep, I stepped out of bed and crept tentatively to the front door. I took a deep breath before putting my hand on the knob. My head was starting to clear and, as I reached for the cold metal, my heart began to pound. My breathing quickened. I closed my eyes to brace for whatever awaited me on the other side. I turned the knob and pushed the door open.

No one was there.

All I saw were the neighbor's houses, some illuminated with Christmas lights. The glow of the town in the distance and nearby streetlights made the stars in the sky faint. The leafless shrubs that flanked my porch looked extra skeletal in the partial light.

"Hello?" I called into the dark. It was quiet, and I didn't see anyone or anything. Not a creature was stirring. Someone, or something, had definitely knocked. What if they're hiding somewhere? I looked from side to side. Dream Jackie's words suddenly echoed in the back of my mind. Is this what she was warning me about?

"Anyone there?" I tried again. By this point, the quiet had gone from peaceful to eerie. I also felt kind of ridiculous, not to mention a little chilly, standing on my porch at 3 a.m. in pajamas. "Okay, then. Goodnight," I said just in case.

I began to back slowly toward the door and was answered with a "Meh" that brought my attention down to a goat walking to the porch from the side of the house my bedroom window was on. It was white with black hooves and had bright green eyes and peculiar horns that curved in an arch backward over its head. They were red with white stripes. White with red stripes? With these horns, it was as tall as my knees. Must be a pygmy goat. Not that I'd call myself a goat expert, but it was strange looking. Something about it seemed almost supernatural.

"Meh!" it bleated again as it reached my side. How did it get into the neighborhood anyway? Did somebody have a pet goat?

"Go home, little goat." I tried to shoo it away, but it just stared at me and blinked those luminous green eyes. Do goats remember where they live?

"Meh."

"Go away." I pointed to the street.

"Meh."

"Okay." I crouched down and stared it directly in the eye. "Go. Home." Again, I pointed in the general direction I wanted it to go, but it didn't budge. It had to have an owner somewhere nearby, right? I tried a different tactic.

"Giddy up." I reached over and slapped its butt.

"Meh..." it responded, almost indignant, with narrowed eyes. Maybe it just needed a push to get going? I gripped its horns and began to apply pressure but only ended up slipping. Once I was on my knees, I lost my grip and let go of the horns. The goat invited itself into the still open door.

"Hey!" I jumped up and sprinted inside after it. Already it had made itself at home and was making a bed out of a blanket that had been relegated to the floor. Once it was satisfied with the arrangement, it lay down.

"Meh."

Smug little goat. I picked it up and set it back on the porch. Problem solved. I had just turned away from the now locked door to go back to bed when I heard tapping again. I rolled my eyes and started walking back to the bedroom. If I ignored it, it would probably go away. Eventually.

"ME-E-EH!"

I froze. It sounded insistent. I really didn't want a goat in the house, but it was going to be hard to block out the tapping and explain the bleating to the neighbors if it was going to continue the rest of the night. On the other hand, maybe one of them would recognize the sound and come get it. But it was also kind of chilly.

I exhaled sharply and opened the door and let the goat back in. It went straight for the blanket, and I bit my lip. It sure as hell wasn't going to be unsupervised in the house the rest of the night, so it would have to stay with me in the bedroom.

"Come on." I tugged the blanket and used it to drag the goat. Once in the bedroom, I closed and locked the door. The goat was lazing contentedly, totally unfazed by the move. In fact, it almost looked like it was smiling. Glaring at it, I climbed back into bed. As I finally lay down and closed my eyes, I really hoped I wouldn't regret this decision.

Next thing I knew, I was standing in the middle of an open field, completely alone. It was night. Stars were twinkling and I could see snow-covered mountains in the distance and northern lights behind them. Very peaceful and serene.

Out of the corner of my eye, I saw a figure moving toward me. As it got closer, I made out a demon. It was wearing a green cape and carrying a bag and chains that rattled rhythmically like sleigh bells. It had yellow eyes and a long, red snake-like tongue. I let out a scream and began to run. The demon spotted me and pursued. I sped up until I reached the edge of a cliff. Without hesitation, I jumped. It was a quick fall, but I jerked to a stop at the bottom and hovered above the ground, which started glowing a nuclear green.

Suspended horizontally, all I could do was watch as the ground rumbled and cracked open.

And then the goat climbed out of the crack and began to stumble toward me.

Suddenly, my vision was filled with only its goat face.

"MMMEEEEEEEEEEEEEEHHH!"

6

Friday, December 18th

My alarm buzzed. Startled, I jolted awake. My heart racing, I sat up to survey the room and didn't see the goat or the blanket. It was just a dream! I rolled out of bed and began my morning routine. I pulled a pair of khaki jeans and a grey sweater out of the dresser and lay them on the bed. As I was changing out of my pajamas, I started reviewing my class schedule for the day and my plans for the weekend in my head.

Lost in thought, my mind wandered to the blanket. The goat may have been a dream, but that was real. I've had it for a couple of years and used it frequently. I thought I had left it on the floor next to the couch but I distinctly remember touching it last night after I had gone to bed. It felt so real. Maybe my dreams were just becoming more vivid?

Creeeak

I jumped. That creak sounded like it was coming from inside. Since I lived in an older house, I was used to strange noises but that doesn't mean they don't catch me off guard once in a while.

I tossed my pajamas into the laundry basket, tugged on my jeans and put on my sweater. I went to my jewelry box and pulled out a silver necklace and matching earrings. While I was putting an earring on, I heard a crisp rhythmic clicking noise. Was it coming from inside the house too? It was probably just the house settling.

At least that's what I was going to tell myself, anyway.

Turning back to my jewelry, I clasped the necklace around my neck. Now for socks.

I finished dressing and realized I could see the hallway directly outside of the bedroom. The door was wide open. When did that happen? I never slept with the door open and don't remember opening it yet this morning. Maybe I didn't close it last night after all. I shrugged and crossed the hall into the bathroom to brush my teeth.

While rinsing, I heard a loud thud from the kitchen. That was a new noise. My eyes widened, and I peeked out of the bathroom door. I spit into the sink, wiped my mouth and moved slowly out of the bathroom. As I went down the hallway, I had a clear view into the living room. There was stuffing exploding from the couch's armrest and remnants of a throw pillow in shards on the ground. What I believed were pieces of the doomed blanket were scattered next to it.

I stopped in my tracks. There were two explanations that immediately entered my mind. Either I'll need some big balls to get rid of that moth, or…

I took a deep breath and moved to the kitchen. I peeked cautiously inside and saw the trashcan spilled all over the floor with the goat happily eating the contents.

It wasn't a dream.

"NOOO!" I don't have enough coffee for this.

"Meh." The goat resumed chomping away. I moaned and went to right the trashcan. Ripping half a cereal box from the goat's mouth, I began shoving the remaining trash inside. When that was finished, I took the bag out and deposited it into a larger trashcan at the end of the driveway. Now that the goat couldn't dig in the trash anymore, it was time to figure out what to do with it. I knew I didn't want to keep it, and I didn't know where it came from, but it probably already had an owner. How else would it have ended up here in the neighborhood?

I began contemplating a drop and run at the local humane society. I didn't have time to search for an owner now, and I sure as hell wasn't leaving it alone in my house all day or taking it to school with me. I know there's a back door at the shelter. I remember that from when I went with Kylie when she brought Sia home as a kitten about three years ago, and I was fairly certain that there was a metal handrail on the side of the porch at the back door that I could tie the goat to. I could leave it there and a worker would find it when they came to open everything up and they'd do whatever they do with animals that came in. Maybe check for a microchip (do people microchip goats?) and put out a lost and found notice.

Deciding that was my best option, I went to a closet where I keep a box of mementos from old boyfriends and retrieved a moderate length of rope. I tied a slip knot at one end, creating a loop. Now, the hard part.

I approached the goat, which was now in the living room slurping up the tattered remains of my textiles like spaghetti. It turned its head up at me and I hid the rope behind my back.

"Hi. Just passing through," I said as I hid the rope behind my back.

"Meh."

I smiled. The goat blinked at me and lowered its head to continue eating blanket strips. If there was any consolation in all this, at least I wouldn't have to clean up as much.

I moved closer to the goat, slowly bringing the rope to my front so it would be ready. The goat was still occupied and had moved from the blanket to the pillow.

This might be easier than I thought.

I took another step toward the goat and landed on a creaky floorboard. That got the goat's attention and I froze, whipping the rope behind my back.

"Meh."

"Still just passing through, nothing to see here."

The goat's green eyes were locked on mine. I shuffled a couple steps to the right and broke eye contact to examine the ceiling. I waited a couple of seconds and looked down to see the goat was distracted once again. It was now or never.

With the rope in hand, I lunged at the goat.

"Meh!" Startled, it backed up a couple inches. In a crouch position, I tripped forward with my arms extended outward and brought it to the ground with me.

"Ha!"

I maneuvered my legs in front of me and now restrained the goat with my thighs and arms, still clutching the rope in one hand.

With only a minor struggle, I slipped the loop over the goat's horns and around its neck. I guided it out to the car and put it in the backseat, hoping it wouldn't try to jump and join me in the front. It was quiet and still as I got into the driver seat, turned the key and began backing out of the driveway.

We got to the humane society without incident, and I pulled around to the back and parked the car. No one else seemed to be here yet, but there was a cardboard box on the porch in front of the door. Maybe an early delivery? I let the goat out of the car and walked it to the porch. The top of the box was open. Curious, I tied the goat to the handrail and went to peer inside. I gasped when I saw a small grey kitten quivering in the corner.

I did not expect that.

Based on the size, it couldn't be more than a couple months old. It didn't seem malnourished and the medium length fur wasn't matted or dull. Someone's cat probably had a litter of kittens and the owner didn't want them. The rest of the kittens must have escaped. Or they were given away. I wondered how long the box had been on the porch.

I reached inside to pet the kitten, but my hand hovered above its silky looking body. I couldn't bring myself to actually touch it. I didn't want to startle it.

I withdrew my hand. The goat watched me intently and pawed the ground as I turned away and walked back to my car.

I was about to resume my commute when my

phone chimed. I pulled it out of my purse to see a text message from Kylie.

Where are you?

I looked at the time. 7:25. Shit! I have students coming in 35 minutes.

I had something to take care of before I came in. I'll be there soon.

K. Remember gift for gift exchange. You did buy one, right? Faculty party today!

The words were followed by snowflake and Christmas tree emojis. Kylie's obsession with Christmas almost puts department stores to shame. I also had completely forgotten about the faculty party. I never actually planned on going. It was just David's way of showing his staff appreciation and team building or something. He also made it clear that it was a *holiday* party, not specifically a *Christmas* party, so he was still technically following his own rule.

Yeah, I'm not going.

Booo! You promised.

Sorry.

"Not sorry," I said out loud. I only said I'd go to get her off my back. I never intended to actually follow through.

No you're not :-P Do it for me?

I could imagine Kylie pouting her lips and making big puppy dog eyes.

Not gonna happen.

Come on. It'll be fun!

Fun...

There's a bar.

I have booze at home.

Come with me. PUH-LEEEASSE?

I thought for a minute. I really didn't want to go. But it is Friday, and what else am I going to do tonight?

Okay, fine.

Yay! Now get to work before you change your mind.

I dropped my phone back in my purse and sped off to the nearest coffee shop. When I walked in, sleigh bells on the door jingled to alert the barista, who looked up and smiled to acknowledge me while she helped another customer. There were a couple of people still ahead of me. I already knew I wanted an iced dark roast, but I glanced at the chalkboard menu behind the counter anyway.

The writing was in red and green with little holly leaves, candy canes, and gingerbread men stickers decorating the empty space. A chalk-drawn coffee cup adorned one corner and in a handwritten flourish next to it I read *Fa-la-latte*. I puzzled about whether it was a drink to order or a cute Christmas coffee pun, and my eyes were drawn to a draping of blue and gold in the opposite corner of the of the chalkboard.

An Elf that Helps toy.

"I can help whoever's next," the barista called.

I walked up. "Hi, I'll have a grande iced dark roast."

"Okay," She tapped the register, and I pulled out my phone. It was already 7:37. "Anything else?"

I eyed the bottled drinks displayed below the register, grabbed an iced coffee at random and set it on the counter. People like iced coffee, right? Perfect for the gift exchange.

"And this."

The barista tapped the register again. "All right. Your total comes to $6.35."

I gave her my debit card and grabbed the bottle of iced coffee as she completed the transaction. She returned the card and receipt when it printed seconds later.

"Your drink will be up shortly. Have a great day." She smiled and the next person in line walked up behind me.

"Thanks. You too." I went to the end of the counter to wait for my drink.

* * *

Somehow, I managed to make it to school and begin the lessons on time. Today I decided that we would start with history. We were going to continue our Revolutionary War unit and talk about George Washington's stay at Valley Forge. Not exactly my favorite subject, but the school board seemed to think it was necessary for some reason. The kids probably never used the information beyond the tests they were given, but I could tell that some found it interesting. So at least there's that.

I was just beginning to describe the harsh snowy conditions General Washington and his troops endured when Aiden James raised his hand.

"Miss Smith?"

"Yes, Aiden?"

"Is it going to snow on the 21st?"

"Huh?"

He pointed to the jumbo-sized calendar I had tacked up on the wall behind me. It was, of course, set to December, and a giant snowflake sat on the square labeled 21. The winter solstice. The first official day of winter.

"Oh. Well…uh…" I looked out the classroom window. The sun was shining, and the sky was blue. It was kind of cool this morning, but it was supposed to hit 60 by this afternoon. The only indication it was winter at all were the bare trees. "I guess we'll just have to wait and find out, won't we?"

Doubtful, kid. No snow days in our future.

"The weatherman on TV says it won't snow any time soon," Olivia Larson said.

"Oh," Aiden said.

"But it *did* snow in Valley Forge in the winter of 1777 and 1778," I said, trying to segue back into the lesson.

Tommy Carter raised his hand, his brown eyes twinkling. "Tommy?"

"When can we go to recess?"

7

Back at Headquarters

Yet to Come, Present and Krampus were seated at a table. Yet to Come and Present were playing chess and Krampus had been tied to a chair with his chain. He rattled in confusion.

"Warum hast du mich gefesselt?"

"We tied you up because you invaded Eliza's dream," Past said, turning to look out the window.

"And you keep trying to get her before you're allowed to," Present added, knocking one of Yet to Come's pawns off the board with his rook.

"Fein." Krampus dropped the chain and focused on the chessboard. Yet to Come used his bishop to take out a knight and Present gasped.

"I miss Jackie," Past faced the other spirits. "I wonder if she's enjoying her new body."

Yet to Come wrote *Yes. It's purrfect* on the wall.

"I'm sure she's feline with it," Present said. He began laughing as Yet to Come held a hand up to the place where his face would be and bounced up and down.

"Cut that out right meow." Past smirked as the others resumed their chess game. Krampus looked wistfully to the window Jólakötturinn had leaped through, a single tear on his cheek.

Yet to Come pointed, and Present turned around. Past was floating and making faces at him. While Present was distracted, Yet to Come moved pieces around on the board.

"Das kannst du nicht tun."

Yet to Come put his finger to what would have been his lips. Krampus gave a heavy sigh and looked toward Present. Present turned around again and looked at the board.

"Hey! You can't do that," he said.

Yet to Come was getting ready to write *Checkmate* on the board but stopped when Elf tore off his goggles and threw them on the ground.

"A BOTTLE OF ICED COFFEE?!"

"Did it have peppermint?" Present asked. Past pursed his lips and shook his head.

"No. She should have just skipped a gift all together," Elf said before he mumbled something about cheap and tacky.

All the spirits gasped as their attention was suddenly directed to the wooden door, where Jólaköt-turinn came crashing through, carrying a flail in his mouth. Yet to Come floated to a wall and pulled down a chalkboard where there were four tally marks. He crossed through them to make five total tallies and Krampus bounced up and down excitedly in his chair.

"Welcome back." Elf patted Jólakötturinn on the side.

Jólakötturinn hissed at Elf, still bitter at him for throwing the flail out the window in the first place, and proceeded to bring the flail to Krampus.

"Woo-hoo!" Krampus cheered when the flail was dropped in his lap. He wasn't the only malevo-lent spirit in the room anymore. Jólakötturinn arched his back and twisted around Krampus's legs, purring. Krampus smiled nervously, watching Jólakötturinn's head candle to make sure it didn't singe his fur. That's when Julbok appeared in the fireplace and walked out to the others.

"Meh."

Elf looked down at the goat. "What are you doing here?"

"Meh."

"She dropped him off at the humane society and he didn't know what else to do." Past went to Julbok and began stroking his back.

"*What?!*"

65

"She tried to get rid of him. She didn't want him around," Present said.

"Obviously." Elf looked at Present with a raised eyebrow and turned back to Julbok. "I hoped your appearance would be enough. You'll just have to try again, but this time we'll give her a hint so she catches on."

"Meh."

"Go wait for her at home. We'll take care of the rest from here."

Past drifted over to re-ignite the fireplace, and Julbok walked back into the flames.

"I really hope she keeps him this time," Past said, looking at Krampus.

"Yeah, we don't want Krampus to get her," Present said.

"That too…" Elf examined his hands, wondering if they were becoming more translucent.

8

Friday, December 18th (continued)

Lunchtime rolled around, and I had just opened up my container of leftover chicken and broccoli at a table in the teacher's lounge when Kylie appeared at my side. Today she was wearing a green turtleneck with a large glittery poinsettia at the center and holding a big red bag with white fur around the opening.

"Poinsettia shirt and Santa bag?" I put the lid back on my container and set my fork on top of it.

"Today we're learning about Poinsettia Day. Go fish!" She grinned broadly as she opened the bag in front of me.

"Do you have any 5s?"

"Ha,ha. Just take your present."

I groaned in mock exasperation and reached into the bag only to pull out an oversize mug with a picture of Santa and some elves. Inside were three packets of hot cocoa mix, two candy canes and some chocolate. The entire thing was wrapped in cellophane and tied with a gaudy gold bow. It was absolutely grotesque.

"Wow! It's…"

"I know!"

"Yeah!" Could I get this into the gift exchange without her noticing? I set the mug on the table next to the container of lunch. My stomach growled at the sight of the food, which was getting cooler by the second.

"I just wanted to do something extra for everyone. I also made cookies and they're next to the microwave."

"Cool."

I reached to open the container again when it occurred to me that she had taken her cat to the vet yesterday.

"Hey, how did Sia's appointment go?"

"Well, I'm still waiting on the test results, but the vet thinks that she probably just has a bladder infection. So, I got some medicated food to try for a couple of days while I wait to hear."

"Aah, okay. That doesn't sound too bad." I picked up my fork.

"Could definitely be worse. I can't imagine not having Sia around." She spotted art teacher Kristy Anderson and music teacher Curt Richter entering the lounge. "I'll see you later. Santa has to pay a visit to some new people."

"Bye."

I put the mug into my purse and went back to my lunch while Kylie skipped off to our colleagues.

* * *

When the school day finally ended, we headed to the restaurant, which was a couple of blocks away, for the district holiday party. The Whattown Elementary group walked together since it was easier than moving our cars the short distance. Kylie next to me practically shouted carols along with everyone else in our caravan.

"Jingle bells! Jingle bells! Jingle all the way!"

All around the mulberry bush, the monkey chased the weasel... I started singing in my head. This happened whenever I heard a Christmas song I wanted to block out. It was basically instinct at this point.

"Singing is the best way to get into the Christmas spirit." We were reaching our destination, and Kylie turned to me with a look that told me I should have been singing, too.

"Because there isn't enough to get you into the spirit already?" I eyed the oversized wreath on the restaurant door.

"*Never.*"

We entered the restaurant and found our way through the main dining area to the private room reserved for our gathering. A bartender leaned behind the bar, across from a couple of appetizer tables along one wall and overlooking chairs set up in a circle at the center of the room.

I began to suspect I would be forced to actually interact with my colleagues and stick around.

Kylie, meanwhile, was focused on the decorations and her face was lit up like the lights that adorned the walls. A waving animatronic Santa waited to the right of the entrance to the private room.

Ho! Ho! Ho!

And it talks. Poncy elf.

"Isn't this amazing?" Kylie beamed at it all.

"Yeah, it looks like the district spared no expense."

There were even token menorah and dreidel decals pinned to the wall. With a few exceptions, the gaudy decor probably all came from a dollar store. I pretended to gag and Kylie hit me on the arm.

"Oh, come on. Where's your Christmas spirit?"

"There, apparently." I nodded toward the bar, where I saw a sign advertising something called a mistletini and other Christmas-themed drinks.

"Ha!" Kylie grabbed my arm and we went to make ourselves merry.

In front of us at the bar, Melissa Taylor, the

Whattown Elementary School Principal and our boss, held a white cocktail in her hand. Her black hair was tied back in a tight bun and she was wearing a white button-up shirt with a navy pencil skirt. Her flashing light-up novelty necklace made her drink glow red and green, and she bent over to brush something off her skirt before moving from the bar and passing us.

"Hello, Kylie and Eliza. How are you both?"

"Great," Kylie said.

"Mh-hm." I managed through gritted teeth.

"I love the decorations. And I'm looking forward to the gift exchange." Kylie grinned and patted her purse, which was bulging with a present.

"Glad to hear it. I hope you were below the maximum cost when you chose your gift?"

"Of course."

Kylie's voice had dropped an octave and she gave Melissa her best *I would never break the rules* look. I snorted and grinned, knowing the truth.

"Wonderful." Melissa stood on tiptoes, shifted a little and raised her glass to the center of the room, presumably at someone in the crowd. "Now if you'll both excuse me. Enjoy the party."

Melissa gone, Kylie and I looked at each other.

"I'm surprised she's drinking," Kylie said. "She's usually so uptight."

"She's wearing a flashing necklace, too. It's a

miracle."

"Next." the bartender called.

Kylie ordered, and I directed my attention to the crowd. Melissa was next to Superintendent David at the wall closest to the appetizer table. Their backs were rigid, and their wide eyes made them look like deer in the headlights. They seemed about as comfortable as two kids at a middle school dance. Everyone else seemed to be enjoying themselves, though. Curt Richter was behind me in line. He laughed with the people behind him and then turned to me, his face glowing red and his smile broad.

"Hey, Eliza!"

"Hi, Curt." I tried to ignore him and watched the bartender mixing Kylie's drink. Curt rested his arm on my shoulder. He didn't seem to care, let alone notice, the side eye I was giving him.

"What does a French composer call a Christmas song?"

"Uh...I don't know. What?" I shifted my shoulder to move his arm off.

"Debussy what I see!" Curt roared with laughter.

"Heh."

Continuing to laugh, he was drawn back to his previous conversation with the other people in line. Kylie appeared at my side with a red drink. It was rimmed in green sugar.

"What'd you get?"

"Mistletini."

"Of course."

"Bah, humbug. Get your drink and I'll meet you by the appetizers." Kylie went to join everyone else.

"What can I get you?" the bartender asked.

"Uh…rum and coke?"

"You got it." He filled a glass with ice and began pouring rum.

Someone had activated the animatronic Santa and the "Ho! Ho! Ho!" was audible as far away as the bar.

"Debussy what I see!" Curt was still in a fit of laughter.

I looked up at the bartender. "Make it a double."

After everyone was served a drink and had the chance to snack on some appetizers, Melissa asked everyone to gather for the gift exchange. We made our way to the chairs in the center of the room and Kylie and I sat next to each other. She gleefully rubbed her hands together before she reached into her purse to pull out a small gift wrapped in silver paper with a red bow tied around it. I felt something tap my lap, where my purse was sitting. I reached into grab the bottle of iced coffee, but as my hand brushed past the mug, I found a flat rectangular gift box wrapped in green paper instead. I pulled it out, making the cellophane around the mug crackle.

I think I know exactly where this came from.

I leaned over to Kylie, who was fluffing the bow at the top of her gift. "You just couldn't resist, could you?"

"What are you talking about?" She looked up from her gift to see the one I was holding in my hand. *"You brought an actual present!"* she practically squealed as she clapped her hands.

"I…"

David made his way to the center of the circle.

"Okay, everybody, quiet down." The buzzing chatter continued. *"Quiet down, everybody."*

Had he always been so much like every nerdy old guy? The monotone voice, the clothes. He even had the white hair and thick-rimmed glasses. His crisp white shirt and pinstriped jacket were both probably starched. Gradually, people began to notice that he was standing in the middle of the circle and trying to speak.

"Thank you. We're going to play musical chairs. Set your gift on the chair you're sitting in. Then the music will start, and you'll walk around the circle until it stops. The gift on the chair you're standing in front of when the music ends is yours."

He sounded just as thrilled as I felt.

The chatter resumed as David left the center of the circle and everyone began standing and setting their gifts on their seats. Then, after a second of feedback from the speakers, the all too familiar notes began to play and Mariah Carey's voice filled the room.

Great. My favorite Christmas song. I hoped Mariah was proud of herself for unleashing it on the world. "Pop Goes the Weasel" began to loop in my head.

We rotated like cattle, galumphing around until the music abruptly stopped. I was standing in front of a chair with a small green bag with gold tissue paper exploding out of it. Everyone began tearing open their new packages. I looked over at Kylie standing to my right with a slightly disappointed look on her face. She had opened a metal container of bacon-flavored gumballs.

"Gag gift." She shook the container, rattling the contents. "What'd you get?" She nodded at the bag sitting unopened on my chair.

"Let's find out." I took out the top layer of tissue paper to reveal a small straw yule goat. My thoughts flashed to the goat that I had dropped off at the humane society. I removed the straw goat from the bag and ran my fingers along the red ribbon wrapped intricately around it, then turned it in my hand.

"Hey, there's something with it." Kylie reached into the bag and pulled out a folded piece of paper. "It's an information card." She handed it to me, and

I began to read it to myself.

> *Yule Goat: The Christmas tradition of the yule goat, or Julbok, comes from Scandinavia. It is believed to have originated with Thor, a Norse God who rode in a chariot pulled by two goats. In one version of the story, the yule goat visited families during the month of December, demanding gifts and treats while making sure preparations for the Christmas holiday were underway or completed. He would remain until Christmas was being celebrated properly. Another version says the yule goat would stalk the countryside on Christmas Eve, frightening children. More recently, the yule goat has become a bringer of gifts, similar to Santa Claus.*
>
> *Yule goats are built with straw, as the last straw from the harvest was once said to have magical properties. This gives the family who owns one good luck for the New Year ahead. Display this yule goat in your home all year long for...*

Blah, blah, blah.

I put the card and the goat effigy back in the bag. Kylie was now deep in conversation with our neighbors, admiring their gifts. Across the circle,

William Brown and Sam Tillman, both seventh grade teachers from the middle school, were seated next to each other where Kylie and I had been. William was pointing to a part on Sam's gift. Sam nodded and comprehension washed over his face. William patted Sam's shoulder and started to open my gift.

Come on!

I willed him to go faster as he delicately pulled apart the paper. I wanted to know what it was that had mysteriously found its way into my purse. He unwrapped a black box and gently removed the lid.

What is it?

He pulled out a large skeleton key with a red ribbon looped around the head. He studied it for a few seconds, then looked around the room. When his eyes found mine, he raised his hand and walked over to me.

"Where did you find this?" He held up the key, relief on his face.

"Uh…" I glimpsed a small tag hanging from the ribbon that said *Santa Key*.

"We don't have a fireplace and my son was just wondering how Santa was going to get in to give him his presents. This is perfect. You just made a five-year-old's Christmas."

"Uh, you're welcome!" I shrugged awkwardly.

What do you know.

That was fortunate.

* * *

I got home after the party and headed straight to the bedroom. I dropped my purse on the bed and casually tossed my gift on top of the dresser while considering who might appreciate a little straw yule goat of their own. As I changed into my pajamas, my eyes registered a glow down the hall from the otherwise dark living room. I grabbed my lunchbox to take to the kitchen, and went to investigate the glow, only to find a pissed-off goat in front of a fireplace with a roaring fire that I don't remember lighting. I dropped the lunchbox.

"Meh…" Its eyes narrowed.

How did it escape from the humane society? How did it get in the house? The door was locked, wasn't it? Anger, terror, confusion, and curiosity each fought for first place as my mind raced. I was angry that the goat was back, scared that it had managed to get in the house, and confused how and why it did. It would have needed thumbs, right?

I looked down its legs and sure enough, it had normal goat hooves.

I didn't want to consider the possibility of someone else being in the house, hidden away somewhere, so I let curiosity win out. I went to my computer and when it started up, I immediately opened the web browser and typed "white goat" into the search bar.

In a matter of seconds, the results numbered in the tens of thousands. I began to filter through, and 32 farming sites, one rapper fan site, five fetish sites, and 23 "goat edition" pop songs later, I came across an article from the online version of the Whattown paper. The headline was bold and read *Yule Goat Burned, No ignition source identified*. As far as the investigators could tell, the yule goat I had watched burn on TV had spontaneously combusted.

Imagine that.

I navigated away from the article and continued trying to find anything that resembled the creature that showed up at my house. Nothing seemed to come close, even when I added "breed" to my search terms. It was obviously some rare kind of goat that even the internet couldn't identify.

Exhausted and defeated, I shut down the computer, and the goat followed me back into the bedroom. As I began to drift off, I thought of Jackie's warning. Maybe it had been more than just a troublesome dream and the goat was the terrible thing she didn't want to talk about. It was kind of creepy that it re-appeared tonight.

"He thought I was you."

He. Was the goat even a boy?

I sat up and grabbed my phone off my nightstand. Using it as a flashlight, I peeked over the edge of the bed to examine the goat lying on the floor.

Yep. Definitely a boy.

9

Saturday, December 19th

S unlight streamed in through the window and I opened my eyes. I rubbed them and began to focus on a large pair of bright green eyes and a face covered in white fur. The goat was standing over me on my bed.

"Meh!"

Not him again. How did he get up on the bed anyway? I never felt anything climb onto the bed or land on it for that matter. Can goats even jump? I didn't think so, but I also didn't think goats had good enough memories to be able to find people after they were dropped off at the humane society. Shows what I know.

He butted me softly on the hip to get my attention. "Meh."

It was eight. In the morning. On a Saturday. Having this goat around was going to get really old, really quick.

I groaned and flipped over on my side, closing my eyes again, but the goat would not be ignored. After a second tap on my hip with his horns, he started chewing my hair. Now I was awake. I moaned and rolled out of bed, sliding my feet into purple suede slippers. The goat blinked at me and bit my pillow instead.

"Oh, hell no." I ripped the pillow away.

"Meh."

The goat leaped off the bed and ran out of the bedroom. I tossed the pillow back on the bed. I should probably follow him and go make sure he wasn't destroying anything else.

I began to trudge to the bedroom door when I had a thought. It occurred to me that the vet's office would accept surrendered animals in some cases, since they had to take them from the shelter anyway to give them medical care. Were they open on Saturday though?

I grabbed my phone off the charger and searched for the Whattown Elementary Veterinary Clinic. I clicked on the "Hours" tab.

Saturday 8 a.m. – 12 p.m.

Good enough.

It was perfect! I never thought I'd be so excited that the vet's office had Saturday hours. And this time, someone would actually be there to take the goat when I left him. I had convinced myself that he escaped the humane society because the slip knot I tied was too loose so he was able to get out and find my house again somehow. I didn't want to imagine it any other way, and besides, I wanted to stay focused on dumping the goat as soon as possible. In a flurry, I pulled on the first pair of pants and shirt I found in the dresser and picked up my purse off the floor. It was heavier than I remembered.

I set the purse on the bed and opened it. The Santa on the mug Kylie had given me yesterday stared out from behind the cellophane with crazy eyes and a comic book villain smile.

I shuddered.

I took it out to the kitchen and shoved it into the back of a cupboard. I'd think of someone to give it to later. For now, at least it was out of sight.

"Meh." The goat looked up at me.

"What?"

I slung my purse over my shoulder, picked up the goat and loaded him into the backseat of the car. Once I was in the driver's seat, I put the key in the ignition and turned it. The radio immediately began blasting "Winter Wonderland". My head went into autopilot.

All around the mulberry bush...

"Goodbye, Dean Martin," I said as I changed the

dial and found a classic rock station. Much better. I proceeded to back out of the driveway, and, out of the corner of my eye, I saw a pair of red and white horns appear from over the backseat, pointing toward the radio. Bing Crosby was dreaming of a white Christmas now.

"Meh." The goat bleated happily.

"Ugh."

I pressed the radio dial again and turned the classic rock station back on. The other song had ended and now a new one was playing *Hell, yes!* I recognized the song immediately and cranked up the volume to sing along.

"Cheap perfuuume!" Eat your heart out Steve Perry. My vocals are on point. Too bad no one else could hear my perfect singing in the car. "Midnight traaain…hey!"

Journey stopped believing so Brenda Lee could rock around the Christmas tree.

"Meh."

I changed the station again.

"STRA-A-ANGERS!" I belted out at the top of my lungs and began swaying back and forth in the driver seat.

"*…was to certain poor shepherds in fields as they lay.*"

"Huh?" The abrupt song change had caught me off guard.

"Meh."

"Ugh."

The rest of the drive continued the same way.

When I arrived at the vet and brought the goat in, there were a couple other people seated in the waiting area. A man with a small carrier containing a cat moved the carrier from the floor to the bench space next to him, and a woman tightened the slack on her dog's leash. The dog wagged its tail and whined, it's interest piqued by the goat.

I was greeted with a confused stare from the vet tech working the front desk.

"Good morning." His eyes followed the goat as we walked toward the counter. "We don't see many goats in here."

"Goat? I thought it was a reindeer."

"Meh." The goat bleated, displeased.

"Uh-huh. Do you have an appointment?"

"No."

"We don't take walk-ins." He checked the computer screen and looked up at me. "But it looks like there's an appointment next Wednesday at four."

"Tempting, but I just want to…er…drop him off." It was a stray goat, but I still felt like I'd be judged for doing this.

"I see."

"It's not mine!" I blurted.

"How did you find it then?"

"It just showed up on my porch. I don't know

where it came from, and I tried to give it to the shelter, but it came back, and..." I stopped. Why did I care what this stranger thought?

"You don't know where it came from?"

"No."

"Or how old it is?"

I glanced at the goat. Not that I'd seen many goats in person, but he appeared to be fully grown. How quickly do they grow? "He's got to be at least a year old, don't you think?"

"Uh-huh. And no indication of any owner?"

"None. Other than the fact that it showed up in my neighborhood." It was still really strange to me. Was it even legal to own a goat in my neighborhood?

"Okay."

The vet tech didn't quite look convinced. Clearly the fact that it was in a suburban neighborhood wasn't enough. I began to worry my shirt hem, getting more and more anxious that he wouldn't take the beast.

"What about those horns. Those can't be natural. Can they?"

Someone had to have painted them. Right?

"Whatever you say." He bent to open a drawer and pulled out a piece of paper. "Once we take the animal, we'll check for a microchip, do a routine physical and try to track down an owner before it goes up for adoption. Here's a stray surrender form for you to fill out."

He set the form on the counter with a pen and I read through. It basically stated that I had found the animal as a stray and was giving up any claim to it. There were blank spaces to be filled in with information about the animal. I uncapped the pen and started filling it out.

Species:

That's easy. *Goat*

Breed:

This was a little tougher. Are there different goat breeds? There probably are, but I have no idea what this one is. *Goat?*

Gender:

Good thing I verified last night. *Male*

After a few more questions, at the bottom of the form, was a line for my signature. I signed and set the pen down on top of the paper.

"There."

"Great."

The vet tech came out from behind the desk with a lead rope. The goat was now nose to nose with the dog standing patiently with its owner in the lobby. The vet tech looped the lead rope around the goat's neck, taking him by surprise, and presumably started walking him to an exam room. I used the opportunity to escape.

I breathed a sigh of relief as I climbed back in my

car. Now the goat was someone else's problem. I turned on the classic rock station and made my way out of the veterinary clinic's parking lot.

As I was driving home, I hit a red light at an intersection near a department store. A visibly pregnant woman and man were trying to cross the street to get to the store. I glanced and saw there was no room in the department store parking lot. It was completely full, and people were coming out with bags almost as quickly as they went in empty-handed. It didn't make much sense, but there you have it. Christmas shopping. I couldn't help but wonder how many of those purchases would be donated or returned in the very near future as the light turned green and I drove off.

When I got home and walked in the door, I looked at the clock on the stove in the kitchen. 11:32. I still had an hour and 28 minutes before lunch with my family. Not that I was counting down and keeping track.

I went back to the bedroom and froze.

The goat was standing on the bed.

His cheeks were puffed up and his mouth was covered in stuffing. It would have been comical if I wasn't so stunned and he hadn't eaten my favorite pillow. He glared at me as he finished chewing.

"*How?*" I breathed.

First the humane society, now the veterinary

clinic. Twice now I had tried to drop off the goat but both times he came back and I didn't know what he wanted from me. There had to be a reason he kept finding me again, and a logical explanation for both escapes…and the fact that he beat me home this time.

The gift bag, still on the dresser, caught my eye. The goat effigy. In a trance, I stared at the living goat in front of me. His horns did look like candy canes…and he had round pupils for eyes instead of those creepy slits goats usually have.

"Meh." He took another bite of pillow.

Then again, maybe he was just a freaky looking regular goat. He certainly acted enough like one. I think. Plus, the yule goat is just a folktale. A story parents tell their kids this time of year to get them to behave…maybe? It's a symbolic thing…isn't it? She'll deny it, but I also bet Kylie dropped that Santa key into my purse. I was sure of it. Mostly. But it couldn't be a coincidence that *I* got the straw yule goat, could it? Every one of those district employees at the holiday party were locals and nobody buys that crap except the few tourists who come to Whattown…probably…and then a goat randomly appears at my house.

And I still don't know what happened to that bottle of iced coffee.

Snapping out of my daze, I practically ran to the

kitchen to get a cookie from the cupboard. *"The yule goat visits families during the month of December, demanding treats and gifts..."*. This would be a good test. Thank God for my sweet tooth.

"All right. Come get your treat!" I called.

The goat's hooves clicked on the floor as he entered the kitchen and looked up at me expectantly. I dropped the cookie, and the goat devoured it with one flick of the tongue.

"There. Now you've had a treat."

"Meh."

He wasn't moving. He just stood there, staring me down.

"Meh."

"No."

"Meh."

"No."

"Meh!"

"No!"

"Meh." He sounded almost...defiant?

"No."

"MEH!" He butted me in the shin with those candy cane horns.

"Ow!" That really hurt. "Fine. One more."

I bent to rub my shin and grabbed the last cookie from the cupboard. The goat gulped it down as soon as it was in front of his face. For good measure, I also offered him an old scrunchie as a gift and this was also quickly consumed.

Nothing happened.

You can imagine my disappointment when the goat not only stayed, but I also lost a scrunchie and was now out of cookies.

10

They Waited

At the Christmas spirit headquarters, Elf stood next to the fireplace talking quietly to Julbok. Yet to Come was projecting *A Christmas Carol* on the screen. It was near the middle, when Present was almost ready to leave Scrooge. Being that he was still chained to a chair, Krampus had no choice but to watch the film. Jólakötturinn set next to Krampus and groomed himself, trying to ignore the film in solidarity. Past and Present were completely engrossed.

It's a little known fact that the Ghosts of Christmas actually appeared to Charles Dickens, and he based the character of Ebenezer Scrooge on himself after what he thought was merely an inspirational dream. The ghosts, of course, were never captured on film, but they loved seeing themselves portrayed by humans nonetheless.

"You know, I wasn't sure what would appear under my robe," Present said as he watched his on-screen self reveal two emaciated children. "They just kind of showed up and I went with it."

"We know." Past rolled his eyes.

"You're just jealous of my adlib skills."

"Mew."

"Uh-huh."

Krampus was unimpressed with the Ghosts of Christmas, in general. "*Zu mindst brauche Ich nicht die ganze nacht für eine Person.*"

"We may need all night for one person, but at least people know who we are," Past said.

"Harrumph." Krampus slumped back as far as he could. He'd be famous again one day. He was sure of it.

Elf watched Julbok walk back into the flames and went to stand behind the rest of the spirits. He cleared his throat and Yet to Come lowered his arm, stopping the film.

"Well, I just sent Julbok back for the second time. She tried to get rid of him again."

Yet to Come wrote *Oh, no!* on the wall.

"Did she catch the hint at least?" Past asked.

"I believe so. But giving her the option to accept him or not was a mistake. Just to be sure she gets it, he's going to follow her everywhere."

"Good idea," Present said.

"Is it though?" Past was doubtful. "Why do we need him to follow her everywhere? We still have five days until we promised to let Krampus loose."

"Right, but…" Elf looked at Past and his eyes grew wide. Jólakötturinn hissed.

"What?" Past was unaware that his flame-like head had begun to flicker.

"*Was ist los?*" Alarmed, Krampus tried to jump but only ended up moving back a couple of inches in the chair. Yet to Come pointed at Past's head with one hand and held the other up to the place his mouth would be.

Past looked frantically to all the other spirits. "I don't know what's happening. Why are you all looking at me like that?"

Staring intently at Past's head, Jólakötturinn crouched down and wiggled his butt, his tail whipping from side to side.

"Your head," Present said. "It's flickering."

"Meow."

"Jólakötturinn, no!" Elf shrieked.

The Christmas cat pounced straight at Past and they both tumbled on the ground, Past landing on the bottom.

"Get off me." He pushed Jólakötturinn, and the cat moved but not before taking a swipe at the flame head again.

Present went to escort Jólakötturinn to a corner.

"Come on."

Past rose. The flickering had stopped, but he still raised his hand to feel the flame. "That's odd. I don't feel sick."

"Gust of wind?" Present suggested, returning to the group.

"What wind?" Past looked at Present. The air was still.

Elf exhaled heavily, and the rest of the spirits looked at him for an explanation.

"Do you know anything about it?" Past asked Elf suspiciously. Elf shrunk as much as possible without actually curling up.

"If we don't make Eliza believe in the true spirit of Christmas, there won't be enough Christmas spirit and we'll disappear," Elf said as fast as he could.

"*Scheisse,*" said Krampus.

11

Saturday, December 19th
(continued)

I was beginning to think the information card that came with the straw goat was a big flaming pile of shit. The treats and scrunchie gift did not work to get rid of the real goat. In fact, he joined me for lunch at my parents' house that afternoon.

"You brought a goat," Nancy said pointedly.

"Yeah, the farm was out of reindeer."

"Meh…"

"Oh." Nancy stared at me. "You brought a goat."

"Where did you get it?" Karen looked at him hesitantly from her seat in a rocking chair next to an undecorated Alberta spruce.

"A farm. I…" I glanced toward my cousin Tim and his baby daughter, Avery, who was sitting on his lap playing peek-a-boo. "I thought it would be fun for the kid."

"At lunch with your family?" Karen raised an eyebrow and wrapped her cardigan tighter around her waist.

"You brought a goat." Nancy couldn't let it go.

Tim turned away from his game to join the conversation. "That's nice of you, Eliza, but Avery just started sitting up on her own."

"I bet your brother would never do something like this," Nancy murmured, smoothing her skirt.

Ignoring Nancy's comment, I walked over to the couch where Tim and Avery were sitting and the goat followed. Upon seeing him, Avery clapped and squealed with delight. "She can still pet him, can't she?"

"I suppose." Tim held her up to the goat and guided her hand to stroke his back. "See? Nice goat."

"Yes. Nice goat." I sneered at the beast. I then noticed that Tim's wife was absent. "Where's Rachel?"

"She got called into work. Doctor's life."

"Aah. Okay."

"She'll be sorry she missed this though." He nodded toward the goat. "Avery loves it."

"Meh."

Avery gave a large toothless grin and cooed as the goat turned to face her. She gripped one of the horns.

"Oh, yes. Poor Rachel, missing the farm animal at lunch," Nancy said.

"Mom," Tim warned Nancy.

"I don't know. He is kind of cute," Karen said, slowly leaning forward to pet the goat herself.

"Lunch is ready." Dad came into the living room from the kitchen and eyed the goat. "I still can't believe you brought that thing. Put the beast outside."

"Gladly."

I heaved the goat into my arms and went to the front door. I turned the knob, kicked the door open and dropped the goat directly outside, slamming the door shut after it. Goat removal accomplished, I made my way to the dining room.

Everyone but Tim and Avery were already seated at the table and Mom was bringing in the last dish, which was a bubbling mac and cheese with a crisp breadcrumb topping.

"Wow!" I said, eyeing it as I took my seat. I love mac and cheese and Mom rarely puts in the time to make it. I was pleasantly surprised to see a giant crock full of it. But in the back of my mind, I couldn't help but wonder. "I thought you were making Hot Dish?"

"I decided since you were coming over, I'd make something special." Mom set the crock right in front of me.

Huh. That was unexpected.

"Well, it looks fantastic." I spooned a heaping spoonful of mac and cheese onto my plate.

"Oh! Frank made his famous jalapeño brussels sprouts." Steve looked down the table at the bowl brimming with bright green. "Pass 'em this way."

"Sure." Dad only managed to touch the bowl before all the dishes on the table shifted a couple of inches, along with the tablecloth. Dad reached a little further to grab for the bowl a second time and watched it move out of his reach again with the tablecloth.

"Is someone pulling on the tablecloth?" he asked no one in particular.

"Doesn't look like it." Tim was placing a freshly changed Avery into a highchair and looked at everyone seated around the table before sitting down.

"Nope," Steve said.

"Okay." Dad tried a third time to lift the bowl of brussels sprouts. This time, the cloth shifted another inch and Nancy's water glass tipped straight into her lap, making an expanding mark on her linen skirt. She gasped and stood to brush the water off.

"What is going on?" Karen asked, holding her glass in case the tablecloth moved again.

I leaned over to see the goat under the table

nibbling a corner of the tablecloth at the opposite end of the table. We made eye contact and he ripped away the corner, sucking it into his mouth.

"Meh," he bleated through a mouthful of linen and walked out from under the table.

"I thought you put that thing outside," Nancy said, looking at the goat as if he was possessed. Which, frankly, he may have been.

"I did." I gave the goat a reproving look.

"Meh."

"How did it get back in?" Mom asked.

"Not sure," I said honestly. Mystery to me.

Nancy dabbed herself with a napkin. "You probably should have just stayed home."

"Or at least left the goat behind," Steve said.

As if I had a choice...

Dad looked apprehensively at the goat. "You know your mother and I have tried to keep animals out of the house since Toby died."

"Meh." The goat walked up to Dad. Dad eyed the goat suspiciously.

Toby was the golden retriever my parents got when I was six. He was the only pet we ever had. He crossed the rainbow bridge 10 years ago. I had honestly almost completely forgotten about him.

"Adam and that dog were inseparable. I remember when it'd snow, Adam would take him out and throw snowballs for him to catch. Toby would get so confused when they'd break on his snout." Mom giggled as she recounted the memory.

"Too bad there isn't any snow out there now. Rachel and I wanted Avery's first Christmas to be white." Tim looked at his daughter in her highchair and bopped her nose with his finger.

"And some people think climate change isn't a thing…" Karen shook her head, making her gold earrings slap her neck.

"It's inconclusive at best," Steve said. "And *if* it's happening, there's nothing we can do about it. It's a natural cycle."

"Exactly." Nancy raised a finger in agreement. "So we shouldn't worry about it."

"Wait." Dad put his fork down. "Even if it's not real, what's wrong with having a cleaner world? Developing renewable resources?"

"Right. But even recycling requires energy and causes pollution." Steve retorted.

"Minimal."

So it begins. Inevitably, there's some kind of debate. I rapped my fingers on the table and looked down at the goat. He was staring at me intently, waiting for some table scraps. I slipped him a brussels sprout and he lapped it up happily. I looked at the bacon bits in the bottom of the bowl and wondered if you could make a kind of bacon with goat meat.

"So obviously we need to have white streets, made of plastic. That will reduce plastic waste and cool cities," Dad said.

"How about we clear the dishes and go decorate the tree?" Mom said. Frank and Tim had now joined the debate about the environment, and it wasn't going to end any time soon.

"I'm surprised you haven't done it already. You're usually on top of these things," Nancy said.

"Yes. But sometimes things get busy in December. Christmas shopping, baking, consoling your sister when she loses her daughter."

Mom placed her hand on Karen's shoulder and Karen leaned on her head onto Mom's hand. With a light squeeze, Mom removed her hand and Karen wiped a tear from her eye. Nancy began twirling her fork in her hand and suddenly became very interested in the ceiling for a second.

"We're all busy. I spent time with Karen too and I still had my tree up weeks ago."

"How nice." Mom started gathering a stack of plates to take into the kitchen.

Hope began to rise in my chest. *The yule goat visited families during the month of December...making sure preparations for the Christmas holiday were underway or complete.* That's why the treat and gift hadn't worked. The goat wanted me to prepare for Christmas. Maybe decorating the tree would get rid of him. That's getting ready for Christmas, right?

"I'm glad you haven't decorated yet," I said. "I'd love to help."

I stood from my seat and the goat followed me into the living room, where we found a small stack of boxes under the tree. They were filled with decorations, of course, so I selected an ornament at random and hung it on the tree.

"There!"

Nancy entered the room with Karen. "The light should always go on first, dear." She set her glass of wine on the coffee table in front of the couch and took the ornament off, putting it back in the box with unnecessary flourish.

The goat butted a different box toward me. I reached into it and pulled out a tangled string of lights. Wonderful. I threw it at the goat and my aunts stared at me in shock.

"It slipped." I gave my best *Oops, I'm so sorry* look and shrugged.

Mom walked into the room and the goat tapped the lights toward me with his horns. I stared down at him.

"Meh."

I looked from the goat to Mom. She looked down at the goat, then to Nancy and Karen, then back at me.

"Do you want to pick them up?"

"I guess…" I bent over and grabbed an end. The string untangled as I pulled upward. My eyes widened as I stood and started to wrap the string around my arm.

"Look at that!" Mom exclaimed.

"They must not have been that tangled to begin with," Nancy said.

"Adam did a good job putting them away last year."

"Don't you want to test them before we untangle them?" Karen asked Mom. I groaned. The loop on my arm was getting bigger and bigger.

"Quasar. 15 points," I heard Dad say in the other room.

"That's a good point, Eliza. We should really plug—"

"Done!" I coiled the last of the string of lights and handed it to Mom.

"Thanks, honey." Mom plugged the lights into an outlet, and they lit up. They were multi-color and Mom's white sweater looked almost tie-dyed in the light. "Great."

She unplugged the lights and started winding them around the tree with Karen. Nancy and I prepared the ornaments.

We lay them on the couch, taking them out of their containers and replacing the little hangers if we needed to. I got into a rhythm and, to my surprise, started to enjoy looking at them. I made it a game. If they were dated, I did the math in my head to figure out how old they were. If they were undated, I guessed when they were made and checked for any indication of a copyright date. Currently, I was searching a box that belonged to a red plastic airplane.

"Uff da!" Karen came stumbling over to the couch, bumping me and knocking the box out of my hand. She caught her breath, leaning on the armrest.

The goat had moved about a foot from where Karen had been seconds before. She had tripped over him as she and Mom were finishing the lights.

"Meh."

I saw the goat eye the airplane box and snatched it up before he could eat it.

"Eliza, are you planning to keep this goat and bring it with you all the time?" Mom cautiously passed by the goat as she strung the last of the lights.

"Well…"

"Is it getting in the way?" Nancy asked sarcastically, bringing a pink plastic rattle with a pink satin ribbon to the tree.

"Eliza, look at this." Mom took the rattle from Nancy and handed it to me. *Baby's First Christmas* was printed on the ribbon in silver.

"Bootylicious is *not* a word!" Steve shouted from the dining room.

"It's cute." I handed the rattle back.

"I remember that Christmas," Mom said as she hung it on the tree. "You lay in your rocker and just stared at the tree for hours."

"Because I couldn't move?" I ventured. *A baby attracted to light and color. Imagine that.*

"Didn't you used to love Christmas?" Karen asked, turning away from the ornament she had just hung.

"Adam always got so excited about the tree and presents and Santa." Mom hung another ornament. "Eliza was a little more hesitant about it."

"Oh, yes, I remember one year you came to visit," Karen said. "You were, oh, eight or nine, I suppose, and you told Jackie that Santa wasn't real."

"Hmm…" My eyes darted around the living room. Where did the goat go?

"Avery! That doesn't go in your mouth!" Tim shrieked.

"Tim spent hours trying to convince her it wasn't true." Nancy watched her son fish a game tile from her granddaughter's mouth. "We missed the holiday parade and meeting Santa at the department store downtown because of that."

"Oh, yeah." It started coming back to me. "That was the year Dad told me I should put out a white Russian for Santa instead of milk. Then we went out for dinner and he ordered a white Russian."

"That's right." Mom sifted through the boxes.

"That's when I knew."

"You were starting to recognize my handwriting on the tags anyway. Adam had already caught on."

"And that means you had to tell Jackie Santa wasn't real on *Christmas Eve?*" Nancy said bitterly. "I'm just glad Nicole wasn't around yet."

"Sorry," I muttered. Can't change the past.

Karen was racked with sobs as she moved behind me. Oh, great. Was she as upset about this Santa thing as Nancy was?

But Karen didn't seem to be paying attention to us. She dropped an ornament on a branch and dabbed her eye with the cuff of her cardigan. Mom and Nancy gathered around her in front of the tree. I could see that the ornament was made of green felt, red sequins and a bow of red ribbon that had been glued on. Inside the wreath was a picture of Jackie, Tim, Adam and me. Adam and Tim were dressed in green overalls with white turtlenecks. Jackie and I were dressed in identical red and white plaid dresses. We were maybe about five years old.

Karen pointed at the ornament. "That was always one of my favorite pictures of the kids."

"It'll be different without her this year," Mom said, rubbing Karen's back.

"Did you ever hear back from the detective?" Nancy was examining the felt wreath ornament and her perfectly manicured red nails stood out against the green.

"Detective?" I took a deep breath. Jackie's death was being investigated?

"Yes," Karen said, ignoring me. "They haven't found anything new. Still can't identify the scratch marks or the brown fur they found."

Scratch marks? Fur? I bit my lip and scanned the room for the goat. Nowhere to be seen. He was probably hiding under the tree behind my aunts and Mom.

"What about the sounds she called to tell you about before she went to bed? The sleigh bells and knocking? Did the neighbors hear anything?" Mom asked hopefully.

"The police finished their interviews with the neighbors. The Johnsons were out of town and everyone else was asleep and never noticed anything unusual." Karen heaved another sob.

"Do they still suspect foul play then?" Nancy asked, putting her hand on Karen's shoulder.

"They're not ruling it out, but because there were no signs of forced entry, they really don't know."

"I see." Nancy pressed her lips together.

"They'll have answers for you soon." Mom nodded at Karen reassuringly.

Knocking and sleigh bells, too? I thought back to the night the goat came. I'd heard knocking in the middle of the night, but no sleigh bells. And the goat didn't have any brown fur...at least that I noticed. So the goat (where was he anyway?) wasn't what Jackie had warned me about. Probably. One thing just didn't make sense though.

"How come no one ever told me about this?" I began to worry the hem of my shirt.

"You didn't know?" Karen looked at me, her small blue eyes still welling with tears and Minnesota accent stronger.

"You never asked," Mom said simply.

"We didn't think you wanted to know." Nancy patted Karen on the shoulder and went back to the boxes of ornaments.

"Oh."

Wow.

I watched in silence while Mom and her sisters emptied the last box of ornaments. After about 10 minutes, they were finally done decorating. The tree looked...as classy as a Christmas tree possibly could. But the important thing is that I hadn't seen the goat since Karen had tripped over him earlier. Decorating worked!

We stood back to admire our work. Karen rubbed some straggler tears from her eyes with her sleeve.

"We're done!" Mom called to everyone at the table. Frank, Steve and Dad emerged.

"Good work, ladies." Dad came up behind me and put his hands on his hips.

"Oh, for cute!" Karen turned around and was

looking at something behind us.

The grin that had taken over my face left as quickly as it had come when I saw Tim come out from the dining room. He was propping Avery up on the back of a begrudgingly cooperative goat.

"Meh."

"OH, COME ON!"

Avery started crying at my outburst. Tim picked her up off the goat. "What?" He looked at me.

"Uh...the rental insurance is void if he's ridden," I improvised. Tim raised an eyebrow and I continued speaking before anyone could question further. "So, does anyone want dessert? Mom, can we make cookies?" Maybe the goat wanted decorations and *homemade* treats.

"Tree decorating and baking? Who are you and what have you done with my daughter?" Mom responded with a sly grin. I shrugged and smiled.

It was worth a shot, anyway.

* * *

That evening, the goat joined me on the couch at home. (No, the homemade cookies hadn't worked, either. But the goat did enjoy the one he got, so there's that.) I was flipping channels on TV and came across *A Christmas Carol*. It was near the middle, after Scrooge was visited by the second spirit and it used his words against him.

"This boy is Ignorance. The girl is Want. Beware them both, and all of their degree, but most of all, beware this boy, for on his brow I see that written which is Doom, unless the writing be erased. Deny it!"

"Have they no refuge or resource?"

"Are there no prisons? Are there no workhouses?"

The booming laugh of the spirit rang out as he dissolved on-screen and church bells banged in the background.

Well, that was needlessly dramatic. It might have been effective in 18-whatever-the-hell when the book was published, but now it just seemed preachy. I rolled my eyes and changed the channel again, trying to avoid anything Christmassy. An impossible task in December, I found. And if you wanted to avoid *A Christmas Carol*, forget it. Most Christmas movies and specials just seemed to recycle the same basic story. Credit where credit was due, though. Charles Dickens struck gold with that one.

I looked at the goat, which was asleep. Maybe if I went to sleep, too?

Supernatural Christmas creatures seemed to like that.

12

Sunday, December 20th

Unfortunately, the yule goat was not an ordinary supernatural Christmas creature. As I suspected I would, I found him in the kitchen the next morning. He was trying to get into the trash can, which was now hidden in a cupboard.

"Meh."

"Yeah, yeah."

I walked to the counter and filled the coffee pot with water and began making coffee. As I watched the brown elixir drop, steaming into the pot, it occurred to me that I had been decorating my parents' house. Of course the goat didn't leave. I needed to get my own house ready for Christmas.

At least I think so.

The goat was either bringing me gifts or expected me to celebrate Christmas and I didn't get anything from him, so that had to be it. It was so obvious!

My excitement was fleeting, though. I thought I had figured out the key to getting rid of the goat but realized that I didn't have any Christmas decorations. I would have to go shopping.

After coffee.

Once I was sufficiently caffeinated and ready to venture out into public, I went to the car and heard a clicking noise when I hit the pavement. I looked down and saw the goat.

He was following me.

"Meh."

"You think you're coming with me?"

"Meh!" he bleated and, with a flash, he was in the backseat of the car. So that's how he escaped the humane society and vet.

Great. Good to know.

"Argh!" I threw my hands out in front of me and took a deep breath.

I wasn't even going to bother trying to put him back in the house because I knew how it was going to end. If I needed a goat chaperone to go shopping for Christmas decorations, so be it. If anybody at the store had a problem with it…well…hopefully they wouldn't.

I gritted my teeth, got in the car, and floored it to the nearest department store. When I got there, there was only one spot left in the back of the parking lot and I came head to head with a dark green mini-van that also wanted it. We both inched forward and jerked to a stop when we realized the other wasn't going to back down. Eventually, I won the battle of wills and the other woman drove off. I took the spot and watched her begin to circle the parking lot waiting for someone to leave.

After I parked, the goat and I walked to the store. Based on the reaction of people we passed, you'd think they'd never seen a goat before. Some kids pointed as their parents yanked them by the hand to keep moving. Curious adults raised their eyebrows.

At the entrance of the store, I was met by a greeter.

"Hello. Welcome to…oh." She looked down at the goat. "You're late."

"Excuse me?"

The greeter grabbed the microphone connected to her headpiece. "Hey, Gary, they're here."

"Who's here?" I asked. A stream of people were going past and bumping into both me and the goat, making it impossible to move. The greeter remained unfazed as she strained to listen to Gary over the hum of shoppers and the automatic doors opening and closing.

"Mh-mm. Yeah. It looks more like a goat, but it'll definitely work."

"What will work? I'm not…"

"I'll let them know." She put down the microphone and pointed to the left. "Okay. So you want to go to Customer Service and ask for Gary. He'll be there in a minute to take you back."

"Great." A path through the shoppers entering and exiting cleared and I walked right past the greeter into the store. The goat followed.

"You really should have that thing on a leash, you know!" she called after me.

"Thanks!" I yelled without looking back.

Instead of going to Customer Service, I fought the throngs of people to get my hands on a miniature fake tree and set of miniature ornaments.

Apparently, I wasn't the only one searching for those things. I finally made it to the seasonal section and it was swarming with even more people than the rest of the store. I felt like a bee enclosed in a hive, having to wrestle my way through to get close enough to even smell the honey at the center.

I was bumped from person to person as I bull-dozed my way toward the center of the crowd where I could see a small selection of mini-trees and mini-ornaments, in a variety of colors. I dove under an anonymous pair of arms reaching for the last set of peacock-themed ornaments and grabbed the first tree I got my hands on. It was in a large plastic tube, about two feet tall, and made of silver tinsel. Next to it was a box of ten glittery pink and purple star-shaped ornaments and I snatched it up. Good enough.

I began my trek back to the registers at the front of the store. Instinctively, I looked down at my feet but the goat was nowhere to be seen. Where did he go? I shrugged. He probably just went back to the car or something. Or maybe just going to the store and choosing decorations is enough to make him disappear? Maybe I wouldn't have to buy anything after all. I felt a weight lift off my shoulders.

That's when I passed the inevitable Santa display.

It was grandiose and elaborate. Strings of lights shone everywhere, and everything was in shades of gold, silver, green and red. Someone dressed as an elf stood at the front of a long line of parents with their children who were waiting to sit on Santa's lap and take a picture. The child currently seated on Santa's lap looked ready to explode into tears. The parents shimmied around in front of the child making exaggerated gestures while Santa made faces to get the child to smile.

Some of the parents in the line looked simply exhausted while their children blabbered on. Others kept looking at their phones and tapping their feet. Others still held their child's hand and gazed at them lovingly while they talked about what the child was going to ask for.

"No. I've told you, you'll shoot your eye out," I heard one exasperated dad say without even looking down at his son. The kid, probably about nine or ten years old, looked seconds away from a meltdown.

Talk about a strong argument for birth control.

To the side of the display, I saw another employee dressed as an elf standing in front of an end cap filled with Elf that Helps merchandise. He matched the Elf that Helps, wearing a blue outfit with a gold applique and trimmed in white fleece with a matching hat. He was staring down at something and looked kind of nervous.

"Go away," he said, gesturing with his arms and moving backward as much as he could. The moment seemed all too familiar.

"Meh."

Thought so. I pushed through the line of waiting people and approached the blue elf. The goat was tap dancing in front of him and seemed really excited.

"Hi. You found my goat. Thanks for watching him for me."

"Oh, thank God. I thought it was part of the display and I was going to have to stand with it all day."

"No, his shift is over."

"It just kind of appeared next to me and started doing this weird tap dance." He looked both confused and terrified. Can't say I blamed him.

"Yeah, he does that. Sorry." I grabbed the goat's

horns. "Bye."

I guided the goat away toward the registers. The little girl on Santa's lap as I passed was reaching up to pull his beard. I stopped to watch the chaos that was about to ensue, but the beard didn't come off. A look of awe filled the little girl.

Real beard. Nice touch. I nodded.

The goat looked up at me intently. He seemed to be watching my reaction but was generally indifferent himself.

"What?"

"Meh."

"Okay then."

The employees at the registers seemed like zombies going through the motions. I just got in line and already there were people queued up behind me. Those poor workers. Better them than me. I watched a couple in one line to pass the time. They had piles of toys on the belt and the woman rifled through her wallet while the man talked to the cashier, who just yawned and blinked. When all the toys had been scanned, the man began bagging the purchases and the woman produced a coupon. The cashier tried to scan it three times, then examined it closely.

"This is expired."

"So? Can't you take it anyway?" the woman asked the cashier.

"No, the system won't accept the barcode. It's no good."

"But they let us use expired coupons all the time at the store on Maple Street."

"Well, they might have a different system that hasn't been updated yet. Ours won't let us take it."

"Look. We have four kids," The man gestured at the toys and placed a stuffed dog into a bag. "Can't you just help us out?"

"Oh, for goodness sake." The customer behind the couple said, a little louder than probably intended. She began tapping her foot and shifted the weight of the board game she was carrying.

"I'm sorry. I can't."

"Ugh. Can we speak to a manager, then?" the woman asked.

"Okay." The frustrated cashier stomped around in a circle and pointed to the name tag, which clearly had *Manager* written on it below the name. "Hello, I'm the manager on duty. What can I do for you?"

I swear the woman's jaw hit he ground and the man dropped the stuffed animal he was holding. I giggled to myself and caught the goat staring up at me.

He threw his head in the direction of the couple. "Meh."

"I can't help them. Their coupon is expired."

"Meh…"

The line I was in went quickly, all things considered, and I made my way back to the edge of the parking lot with my purchases a mere 30 minutes later. I waved to the woman in the green mini-van I'd beat out for the parking space earlier as she drove past me in the opposite direction. Relieved to be done shopping, I climbed into the car after I loaded my purchases and the goat into the backseat.

Back at home, I set my bag on the couch, pulled out the mini-tree and waved it in front of the goat's face.

"See? I'm decorating." I set the tree on the corner cabinet next to the couch and pulled out the ornaments and quickly put the entire box on the tree. Satisfied, I took a step back to admire my work.

"There!"

"Meh."

Everyone's a critic. To be fair, it did look like a fuzzy silver monster with purple and pink spots, but it was my silver monster with pink and purple spots. And shouldn't the goat be gone by now? I decorated my own house, I gave it treats…what else could it possibly want? I sighed, collapsing on the couch.

My phone chimed. I picked it up and saw a notification.

24 hours until End of Year Performance Review

Thank you, phone alarm. As if the end of the weekend wasn't already bad enough, this reminder that I had to see Melissa tomorrow just made it that much more of a bummer. Performance reviews always make me anxious even though I don't have anything to be worried about. At least it was going to be a short week. The kids only had school through Wednesday, which was a half day.

The goat joined me on the couch and pressed the TV remote with his front hoof. The TV lit up and on the screen was *A Christmas Carol*. Again.

I looked at the goat and wondered if I should actually pay attention to the movie this time. Scrooge managed to get rid of three spirits in one night. Maybe I could pick up a few pointers.

I grabbed a blanket and curled up underneath it, relegating myself to the couch for the rest of the afternoon. After Scrooge underwent a change of heart for the millionth time this year, Jim Carey transformed into the Grinch. As the movie started, I was hit with the sudden realization that pretty much every Christmas movie has a miser who changes their mind.

What an obvious trope.

By the time the Grinch was singing about how mean he was, I had fallen asleep. A loud thud from outside woke me up. It was muffled and probably just one of the neighbors doing something, so I dismissed it.

The goat's head cocked with interest and I began to hear sleigh bells.

Were they part of the song?

I thought they might be until they got louder. They were definitely coming from outside. I pulled the blanket farther up thinking of what Karen said what Jackie had heard before she died. The bells went quiet, but the goat stood up.

Then, there was a loud knock on the door.

My eyes widened in horror. I wasn't sure I wanted to answer. Between the story about Jackie's death and getting a goat the last time I answered the door, I was kind of gun-shy.

The goat jumped off the couch, leaped to the door and looked at me expectantly.

"Meh."

Another knock. I shook my head and drew the blanket up even farther.

"Meh." The goat narrowed his eyes and lowered his head.

"Okay."

Apprehensively, I got up off the couch.

My heart beat faster with every step closer to the door. I drew a deep breath before I turned the handle and opened it. A tuner blared out, followed by voices joining it. Instantly, I regretted my decision to answer the door.

"On the first day of Christmas, my true love gave to me a partridge in a pear tree."

Carolers. Seven of them, all dressed in ambiguous, decade non-specific 19th century outfits, singing one of the worst Christmas songs. Who the fuck gives birds and other people as gifts?

The monkey chased the weasel...

The goat looked up at me.

"Meh."

"On the fourth day of Christmas, my true love gave to me four calling birds, three French hens…"

They were only on day four. This song was so repetitive. Really, all Christmas music was. It's just new versions of the same 10 songs over and over. I gritted my teeth and wondered how much of my time they'd waste. God, I hoped they'd be done after this song. I can't stand Christmas music in general, but listening to an amateur performance…yikes. Behind the alleged singers, an audience had started to gather in my yard.

"On the sixth day of Christmas my true love gave to me six geese a laying, five goooooooooooolden riiiiiings…"

And I was done. I slammed the door, locked it and went back to the couch.

The goat looked perturbed, but I couldn't make it through six more days, let alone face the risk of the carolers starting another song.

Over *The Grinch*, I heard the carolers had moved next door and were now threatening the neighbors with squatting if they didn't get figgy pudding.

13

While Julbok Was On Earth

lf was watching through his goggles and the Ghosts of Christmas were playing charades with Krampus and Jólakötturinn. It was Past's turn and he just floated in place in front of them as they guessed what he was trying to be.

"Obelisk?" Present tried.

"No." Past shook his head.

"Skyscraper."

"Nope."

"Mew."

"Uh-uh."

Yet to Come carved *Grandfather Clock* into a piece of wood he was holding for the purpose of playing the game. Past smirked.

"No."

"Empire State building?"

"Nuh-uh."

Pillar Yet to Come guessed. Past shook his head and Krampus sighed.

"Bottle?"

"Mew."

"No, no."

"I give up." Present was perplexed.

"*Es ist eine Kerze*." Krampus would have strangled Yet to Come and Present if he wasn't still chained to a chair. It was so obvious.

"Candle! That's it." Past pointed at Krampus, and Krampus rolled his eyes. "Whose turn is it next?"

Past joined the others and Yet to Come took his place. He held up one arm and pointed upward with an index finger as Elf removed his goggles and turned to the other spirits.

"Statue of Liberty," Elf said as he walked up to the others. Yet to come lowered his arm, his head hanging down.

"What did you see?" Past asked.

"Julbok got Eliza to go to the store and pick out decorations."

"*Wie schön*," Krampus scoffed. He would have crossed his arms if he could.

"It is nice. We want her to get in the Christmas spirit, remember?" Past hit Krampus on the back of the head.

Jólakötturinn hissed and batted at Past, so Yet to Come etched a square on the floor. Jólakötturinn's ears pricked up and he tentatively walked over to the square, climbed into its boundaries and lay down, his front legs folded under his chest.

"And she did it of her own free will," Elf said.

"Do you think it will work?" Present asked.

"I'm not sure. She seemed kind of apprehensive about the whole thing."

"Well, it's a start anyway," Past said. "Decorations might make her feel festive and that might make her feel more generous."

"Why can't we just tell her what to do? Or make her do it?" Present wanted to know.

"She has to do it on her own," Elf reiterated. "We can give her hints, but if we tell her outright what to do or make her do something, it's not genuine."

"So, it has to be genuine. Even if she does it, if she was forced we'll disappear?"

"Yep."

"What about Julbok? If the rest of us disappear, will he disappear too if he's still on Earth?" Past asked.

"Yes," Elf said.

Oh dear, Yet to Come etched into the wall.

"Was machen wir?" Krampus asked.

"Nothing. We give her hints and have to hope she catches on quick," Past said.

Yet to Come raised his hand and held up three boney fingers.

127

"We only have three days left!" Present exclaimed.

"But a lot can happen in three days," Elf said, trying to sound convincing as Yet to Come lowered all but his index finger and pointed at Past, whose head had begun to flicker again.

Past began feeling around his flame. "Damn it."

Elf looked at the fireplace, wondering what it might take for Julbok to get Eliza to remember the true spirit of Christmas. He then watched as Present and Yet to Come pumped bellows at Past's head to reinvigorate the flame.

Past...childhood...Christmas during childhood...

As the flame stabilized, Elf snapped his fingers and pointed upward.

"I've got it!"

"Got what?" Present asked, returning the bellows to the fireplace.

"An idea." Elf grinned tentatively.

"And? What is it?" Past asked, running his fingers through his flame.

"What's Christmas without a little snow?"

14

Monday, December 21st

The next morning, I got to work as usual. It was a completely normal Monday morning. I was hanging out in my classroom at my desk, the goat standing next to me, you know. He followed me out to the car again when I left the house and hitchhiked with me. No big deal. It's perfectly acceptable for a teacher to have a goat with them in their classroom. Hopefully none of my students are allergic to farm animals.

Just imagining the legal trouble made my eye twitch.

I looked at the goat and sighed. I couldn't figure out why he would come with me. What could I possibly do to celebrate Christmas at school? Even if I wanted to, I was strictly forbidden from doing anything Christmas-related with students. As long as they were here, my hands were tied. Trying to focus on anything else, I turned on the computer.

Just as I was started updating myself on the latest news, the warning bell rang and Tommy Carter was the first student to come in. Naturally, he noticed the new classroom addition right away.

"What a funny-looking reindeer," he said as he took off his backpack.

"Meh."

"Can I pet it?" He walked up to get a closer look.

"Uh, no, Tommy. I don't think so."

"Wow! Miss Smith brought a reindeer!" Olivia Larson walked in with Aubrey Moskowitz and they looked at each other with big, excited smiles.

Aubrey didn't even bother to put her backpack down. "Let's go see!"

"Hey, girls, I just told Tommy that we aren't going to pet the reindeer..."

"Meh."

"Er...goat."

By then the other 27 students in my class had started flowing in. Once they caught sight of the goat, all hope was lost. They were irrevocably distracted. They were all buzzing with excitement at the side of my desk by the time the bell rang to signal the official start of the school day.

"Meh." The goat was trying to escape the cascade of little hands and looked panicked.

"Okay, guys, I think it's time to take your seats."

As the chatter continued, I clapped my hands to get their attention.

"EVERYBODY GO SIT DOWN!" I shouted. Not in a mean way, but in a strict, I'm the teacher and you'll pay attention kind of way.

This worked, and everybody was sitting in their assigned places within a minute. Good. Now I could begin the lessons. Again, I started with history and continued with the American Revolution. Today we discussed Loyalists and what it was like to be one in the colonies. I kept eyeing the goat periodically. He was sleeping under my desk.

After an hour or so of talking about dead white guys and how they treated those who disagreed with them, we moved on to math. By this point, the students were restless, and I could tell they were checked out. They were staring out the window or watching for the goat to reappear. Obviously they were as ready for winter break as I was.

"So, does anybody remember what we call it when we cut our pizza into four equal pieces?"

We were learning fractions and I thought this was pretty basic. They seemed to understand last week, but no one was raising their hand today.

"Anyone? Four equal pieces?" Due diligence. For my own edification, I have to ask twice before moving on. This time, Aubrey Moskowitz raised her hand. See? It works once in a while.

"Aubrey?"

"Miss Smith, can we go outside?"

I looked out the classroom window. Again, the sun was shining, and the grass was still mostly green. I had to admit, it was inviting and I wanted to go enjoy it. But alas, we were stuck in the classroom until lunch and recess.

"Not right now. But we've only got two hours until recess." Two hours? Haven't we already been here for six? Ugh. Longest day ever. "So, does anyone have—"

That's when I heard a metallic clunk. The goat had woken up and his horns hit my desk drawer.

"Meh."

The drawer began to rattle and suddenly shot open. I heard a thud and saw that one of the *#1 Teacher* snowmen that was holding a sled had fallen out onto the floor. I knew I should have donated them to the thrift store earlier. That's what I get for procrastinating.

"Excuse me. I'm just going to…"

I bent over to pick it up, but before I could it stood up and shook itself off. I quickly pulled my hand back. It looked up to the drawer, where another snowman, this one holding a pair of skis, was walking on the edge. The first snowman whistled and gestured. A chain of snowmen followed, and soon there were 32 *#1 Teacher* snowmen on the floor. They marched to the center of the by-now squealing classroom and pounded the accessories they'd been holding on the ground in unison. They then froze and, as we all watched in amazement, exploded one by one like fireworks. Seconds later, I felt a wet, cold drip on my hand.

It was snowing.

The snow was falling hard and fast and already there was at least an inch or two on the floor. The snowmen were gone, but their accessories remained and had grown to human size.

Aubrey was the first to hop on a sled. Olivia got up, gave her a push, and hopped on the back. They glided across the floor and giggled uncontrollably when they softly hit the wall. My students erupted in cheers. Tommy threw a snowball at another student, and before I knew it, the classroom was mayhem.

I watched the chaos as I tried to figure out what to do. This was definitely not covered in any of my student teaching or education. I was also pretty sure there weren't any procedures in place in the Whattown Elementary Teacher Handbook, either. It was safe to assume this was a first. And none of the kids had winter jackets. Did they need them if they're inside? What about the water damage? Oh my God. How was I going to explain this to the custodian? Or Melissa? Maybe this was all just a dream. I worried my shirt hem and bit my lip.

"Miss Smith, duck!" Tommy shouted as a rene-gade snowball flew toward my head.

As it made contact, the entire classroom fell silent. I stared at them all blankly, thoughts of how to best approach the situation beginning to fade. There was snow, in my classroom, and one of my students just hit me in the head with a snowball. This is what my life had become. I looked at the goat and then reacted the way any rational person would.

"SNOWBALL FIGHT!" I screamed as I made a snowball and pelted it out into the students. They cheered and took cover by their desks.

Snowballs and laughter flew through the air. I even found myself smiling and laughing as I stood to toss another snowball out and crouched behind my desk again. I figured I might as well enjoy it since there was nothing I could do about it. Aiden James joined me as I formed a new snowball and stood to throw it.

"Miss Smith, it's snowing."

"Mh-mm." I smiled. I had forgotten how much fun snow was.

"The calendar was right." He pointed to the jumbo calendar where the snowflake marked the 21st. Today.

A cold jolt went through my body. "Yeah."

"Meh!" The goat seemed particularly excited as

he wandered back behind the desk with us. I patted him on the head and the shock I felt for a second switched to exuberance. I finished making another snowball.

When I stood to throw this one, my eye caught movement in the window on the classroom door. Principal Melissa moved back in front of the window and stared inside. Her jaw was probably hitting the floor. I know my jaw did as I dropped my snowball.

"Oh, no."

Dodging both snowballs and students, I ran to the door and stepped outside with a little pivot. *Please don't let her be mad, please don't let her be mad, please don't let her be mad.*

"H…hey, Melissa! How are you?"

"Eliza, what is going on?"

"Uh, learning about weather?"

"Uh-huh." She looked in the door window again and the goat bleated as he hopped in the middle of the classroom. "And the goat?"

"It's…a long story."

Melissa watched the kids running amok in the classroom for a second, then turned briefly back to me, back to the kids, and finally stared me dead in the eyes.

"Clean it up by this afternoon, and it might not come up in your performance review."

She turned sharply on her heel, making the bottom of her blazer fly out a little, and walked off with unnecessary intensity. I fell back against the classroom door, relieved. That could have been worse. After a deep breath, I turned around and went back into the classroom. As you became more and more experienced as a teacher, you'd think you'd seen everything. Then you'll have a moment that proved you completely wrong. I don't think anything will ever top an indoor blizzard.

I had my students help clear out the classroom by throwing snowballs out the window. It was still warm enough, they'd melt fast. And I'd ask the custodian to bring a big mop and dehumidifier to run overnight. That would take care of the excess moisture…I think. The only thing left was the snowman accessories. For the time being, I propped the sleds, skis, snowshoes, etc. against the wall but eventually I'd have to have a bonfire or something.

* * *

The end of the school day eventually came, and it was my turn to usher the students to the buses. The goat trailed behind as I followed my class out the door to Kylie's classroom where we waited for her students to join us. I smiled and waved as she dismissed her children and began gathering things from her desk to leave. She was wearing an oversize pale blue sweater with silver flecks and a large silver snowflake at the center with offensively shiny silver leggings. I guess she was channeling the Snow Queen today. In contrast, I was wearing a black turtleneck with a black knee length skirt (with pockets!) and black boots. I shot Kylie a quick text before her room completely emptied.

Love the outfit.

She picked up her phone and gave me a sneer before typing.

Thanks, I like yours too. Who died?

I scoffed as I put my phone in my pocket and resumed my walk to the entrance of the school where the buses were lined up outside. As soon as the river of pupils ebbed, I made my way to meet Melissa in her office for my performance review.

Even though I knew it would probably be just fine and I had no reason to be concerned, I still felt like a kid who had been called to the principal's office. Literally. I paused in front of her office and took a deep breath. I opened the door and walked in to find Melissa on the phone. She looked at me and held her index finger in the air.

"Yes, I understand. Mh-mm." She shifted her eyes from side to side and bobbed her head.

I took a seat in one of the chairs facing her desk and the goat stood next to me. I could see

Melissa's foot tapping below her desk. Next to her computer, I caught sight of an Elf That Helps. It was propped up against the computer monitor. I raised an eyebrow. Seriously. I never see them and this year they're everywhere. Is there a clearance sale somewhere?

"I know…yes, I'm…Okay, Mom…yeah….I'll look…okay. I've got to go. Bye." She hung up. "Ugh. My apologies."

"No worries."

"My mother wants to find my father a gift for Christmas and she's having quite a difficult time. I've heard about it every day at least once since the end of November and, frankly, it's exhausting."

"Uh-huh."

Melissa rested her elbow on her desk and massaged her temple for a second before grabbing a stack of papers and shuffling through them. She was usually so rigid and organized, it was almost refreshing to see her a little frazzled and caught off guard. She didn't even seem to notice the goat.

"But we're not here to talk about that, are we?" She grabbed a piece of paper from her stack and set the rest down on her desk. "So. Your performance review."

Composed once more, she began skimming over the paper. I stared anxiously at her, hoping she'd want to talk more about her parents and that gift instead. My heart was almost beating out of my chest as I willed her to go back to her mom. I clenched one of the goat's horns a little too hard.

"Meh."

Oh, no. I let go of the horn. Melissa eyed the goat and looked at me critically.

"Is it going to be here for our entire conversation?"

"I paid for the rental until 6. Might as well get use out of it, don't you think?" I smiled apologetically.

Melissa was not amused. She scowled and I could feel the judgement radiating from her.

"All right. You're never late and you don't abuse your leave. For the most part your students are performing where they should be, and their parents typically have good feedback after conferences."

"Okay."

"You work well with your colleagues and tend to stay out of office politics."

"I like to think so."

"I feel obligated to let you know, however, that if your lessons continue to become any more creative, we will have to take disciplinary action."

"Creative?" Now I was confused. I thought making lessons fun was part of a teacher's job. I also wasn't doing anything the other teachers weren't. Was this about the snow?

"Yes. Causing damage to the floors and endangering the students. Bringing that…" she gestured toward the goat.

"Meh."

Yep. This is about the snow. *Why didn't I get rid of those snowmen while I had the chance?*

"You're lucky nobody was injured. Any more stunts and you'll be suspended for the rest of the year without pay."

"But I—"

"Just make sure it doesn't happen again and you have nothing to worry about. Okay?"

I didn't know what to say. Melissa just stared at me. "Okay."

"Now, if you'll sign this."

She handed me the paper copy of the review with a pen. I set it on her desk and signed.

"Thank you for meeting with me." She looked back at her computer screen and began typing. "I'll see you in the morning, then."

Seething, I stomped through the hallway, trying to lose the goat. Of course, he caught up and butted me softy on the back of my calves. Was he trying to apologize?

"Meh."

"This is all your fault." I stopped to spin around and face the goat, right in the middle of the school hallway.

I tried to give him a chance at finding a good home

twice. When that didn't work, I took him in and tolerated him. He'd been nothing but a nuisance since he showed up. I looked up the number for animal control on my phone and dialed.

"Hi, I'd like to report a stray goat at Whattown Elementary."

15

Things Steadily Grew Worse

While Elf was wearing his goggles and watching Julbok on Earth, the Ghosts of Christmas circled around him with Jólakötturinn. Krampus was still chained in his chair and had been positioned to look out a window. The others were riveted as Elf narrated the goings-on in Eliza's classroom, but Elf had gone silent once he watched Eliza walk into Melissa's office for her performance review.

"Those poor snowmen." Present looked down and took the holly crown off his head and held it at his chest. Yet to Come patted him on the back.

"Mew."

"What happened? Did it work?" Past brightened.

"Uh, kind of." Elf took off the goggles and pocketed them.

"What do you mean *kind of*?"

"She almost got fired and called animal control to pick up Julbok."

"I knew it was a bad idea for him to follow her everywhere." Past said. "Did animal control take him?"

Julbok appeared in the fireplace and walked over to join the other spirits. "Meh."

"Guess so." Present bent to pat Julbok on the head.

Ich wusste dass es nicht so wre. Ich hasse den Schnee. Krampus appeared next to the other spirits and chucked Jólakötturinn under the chin. Jólakötturinn began to purr loudly.

"It could have worked. Just because you hate the snow doesn't mean everybody does, Krampus." Past rolled his eyes. *"Krampus?"* Past looked in shock at Krampus, who was now right next to him.

"You should be chained up," Present said, straightening from patting Julbok.

"Meh."

"Present! Your face!" Elf screamed. "It's wrinkling."

Present, who had smooth, youthful skin, had begun to develop shallow crow's feet around his eyes and frown lines on his forehead. He felt around and could make out the wrinkles with the tips of his fingers.

"My beautiful face!"

"Calm down." Past produced a small glass tub of

face cream and handed it to Present. "Here. Use this."

Present applied the face cream and dropped the container before slapping both palms on his cheeks.

"Aah!"

"Yeah, it can burn a little." Past picked up the container and stored it. The wrinkles on Present's face disappeared as he shook his head to alleviate the sting.

"Now that that's taken care of, Krampus…how did you get up?" Elf turned to Krampus and Krampus shrugged.

"Die Ketten verschwanden."

"The chains disappeared?" Past asked. Yet to Come pointed and all the spirits looked toward Krampus's chair. There were no chains anywhere around it. They had, in fact, completely vanished.

"Oh, this is not good," Elf said.

"Mew."

"Meh."

"What does it mean?" Present asked.

"It means that Eliza's still not remembering the true spirit of Christmas and we're starting to vanish. I think we've been going about this all wrong, but we can fix it." Elf bent to whisper in Julbok's ear. "Got it?"

"Meh."

"Okay. Go back and wait for her at school. We

want her to have a little space this time." Elf pointed to the fire still burning in the fireplace.

"Meh." Julbok walked back into the flames and disappeared again.

"What is Julbok going to do?" Present wanted to know.

"Instead of trying to make her feel festive and hope she starts feeling generous, he's going to give her an obvious hint. Then we hope she understands and does it on her own."

"Good," Past said.

"I think so…" Elf looked at Past and his eyes widened. He cleared his throat and pointed at Past's head, which had begun to flicker.

"Not again." Past groaned. Yet to Come and Present went to get the bellows. Jólakötturinn followed, batting at their flowing robes.

Elf looked at Jólakötturinn. "I should have just let you eat her."

16

Tuesday, December 22nd

Tuesday morning, I arrived in my classroom as usual. The only evidence that anything had happened yesterday was the abandoned snow paraphernalia against the wall and humming dehumidifiers. I had to remember to thank the custodian later. He had really come through. It was dry as a bone and smelled vaguely of bleach, so he even took precautions against the possibility of mold. After looking the room over, I turned to my desk and glimpsed a white furry spot under it. Sure enough, when I went to look, the goat was there.

"Meh."

"Ugh." I should have known this was going to happen. Animal control had been worth a try, anyway.

Apparently, I still wasn't celebrating Christmas

right. At the moment, though, that was the least of my worries. First, I had to hide the goat so no one would notice he was back. That would have been a lot easier if he hadn't come out from under the desk when Kylie walked into the room.

"Oh my God!" Her jaw dropped when she saw the goat standing to the side of my desk. "It's true."

"Uh-huh."

The funny thing about kids (adults, too, I guess) is that they talk. When something out of the ordinary happened, like snowmen exploding and creating a blizzard in the classroom, for example, word tended to get around. My class wasted no time telling the rest of the school about the goat and snow day. I was in danger of losing my job and was being haunted by a deranged yule goat who wanted me to celebrate Christmas, but hey. At least I was the cool teacher now.

They probably also told their parents. I was sure I would have more emails and voicemails than usual, and I was dreading having to go through them. Johnny failed a test or Susie bit another kid? The parents would deal with it later. The teacher brings a goat and their kid had an indoor snowball fight? They wouldn't hesitate to reach out immediately. Go figure.

"I didn't believe it when I heard it, but I guess I should give those kids more credit." Kylie leaned over to pat the goat between the horns. "How'd you get it in here?"

"Through the door." I began creating a cave around my desk by moving a snowman sled between the front legs.

"Smart ass. Where'd you get it?"

"A farm."

"Meh."

"Someplace nearby?" she asked.

"Kinda."

"Its horns look like candy canes," Kylie said. "How'd you get Superintendent David to agree?"

"David…doesn't know." The sled at the front of the desk fell over. "Damn it!" I propped it up again. I was being hopeful that Melissa hadn't mentioned anything to David. As far as I knew she hadn't but honestly, I had my doubts.

"Oh." Kylie considered this for a second and gave a sly smile. "Well, I'm sure your class enjoys it."

"They do. He almost got me fired yesterday." The sled was sliding down again. Was there anything I could use to hold it up? I scanned the classroom.

"Why'd you bring it back?"

"I paid for a two-day rental. Perfect!" I moved one of the dehumidifiers to the side of the desk and positioned it in front of one side of the sled.

"Oh." Kylie didn't quite seem satisfied with my response but didn't press further.

148

I looked at the clock: 7:46. Students were going to start coming any minute and I needed to stash the goat. I grabbed his horns and tried to steer him under the desk. "So, did you need something?"

"Not really." She seemed kind of distracted and I noticed her outfit was a simple purple blouse with a pair of dark blue jeans. No Christmas or winter theme today. Something was off.

"Are you okay?"

"Yeah…I just…I'm supposed to get Sia's test results back from the vet today and I'm a little on edge."

"Ah. How's she doing?"

"Still peeing everywhere and getting more lethargic. Her fur is duller too but that could be because of the medicated food."

"When are you supposed to hear?"

"Anytime between now and when they close at 7."

"Hmm. I'm sure she'll pull through. Right now though, I really have to get ready for my students." I looked back up at the clock and then at the goat, which had come out from under the desk.

"Me, too." Kylie seemed kind of sullen.

"Bye."

"See you later." Kylie walked out of the room.

I picked up the goat, shoved him under my desk and placed a second sled in front of the two back legs of the desk just in time for Aiden James to walk in.

"Meh," the goat bleated from his cave.

I kicked the side of the desk, hoping to quiet him. Aiden perked up as he set his backpack on his chair. He watched me, his head cocked. "What?"

"Good morning, Aiden." I smiled.

"Morning, Miss Smith."

The rest of the students came into the classroom and began taking their seats as they excitedly rummaged through their backpacks. Tuesdays were show-and-tell days, and they loved getting to see everyone else's stuff. They got public speaking experience and presentation practice, and I got to sit back and enjoy not having to teach for about half an hour.

Once all the chatter died down, I walked to the front of my desk to officially begin the day.

"All right, everyone. Who wants to go first for show and tell?"

A few students raised their hands. When that happens, I usually select the first student I make eye contact with. This morning, that was Olivia Larson.

"Olivia, come up and get us started."

Olivia grabbed a stuffed giraffe from the corner of her desk and walked to the front of the classroom where she began talking about her family's trip to the San Diego Zoo. I returned to sit behind my desk and pulled the top of the sled out slightly to check on the goat. He was sleeping soundly. Good.

"Thank you, Olivia," I said as she walked back to her seat. "Who's next?"

Tommy Carter's hand shot up and I nodded to him. He reached into his backpack and pulled out an Elf That Helps toy.

Another one? I've seen more this year alone than I have in my entire life.

"This is Rocky, my Elf That Helps. He watches me and my brother and sister and tells Santa if we've been good or bad and what we want for Christmas. My mom said that he's the same age as me and he moves to a different spot in the house every day. This morning there was a note saying that he wanted to come to school with me."

Ha! Tommy's mom was out of ideas and this was an easy solution to get out of moving it for a day. Smart woman. I wondered if the elf had followed his brother and sister to school, too.

"Thank you, Tommy. Who wants to go now?"

"I do!" Samantha Anthony's hand went up. "I have my mom's cactus toy."

Oh, no.

She reached into her backpack and I practically leaped to her desk to stop her before she could pull it out.

"Hey, Samantha, we don't need to see it. Thank you for bringing it in, though." I smiled.

"Okay…" Confused, Samantha dropped the toy in her bag and sat back down.

Phew. I went back to the front of the classroom.

"All right. So, who else has something to share?"

"Me!" Aubrey Moskowitz waved her hand wildly. Before I even had the chance to call on her, she was skipping to the front of the classroom with a doll in hand.

* * *

After the school day ended, I had gathered enough courage to respond to the parent emails and voicemails and already decided to tackle emails first. That would give me a chance to see what kind of concerns or questions they had and figure out a response before actually speaking with them. The goat still corralled under my desk, I took a deep breath and opened my inbox: 19 new messages. Not as bad as I thought it would be. I could do this. I clicked on the first one from Aiden James's dad, Carl. It was time stamped last night.

> *Good Evening Miss Smith,*
>
> *Aiden came home from school tonight talking about a goat and a snowball fight inside the classroom today. He made it sound like there was a real goat and snow in the*

classroom. Since that's not possible, I would
like to know exactly what happened so I can
figure out what he's talking about
    Carl James

Okay, that wasn't so bad. If this is what they're all
like, I can write one generic response to all of the
emails and copy and paste it. I opened the email
from Tommy Carter's mom, Lydia next.

Hi Eliza –
    Just wondering about something Tommy
said when he came home this afternoon. He
told me there were snowmen that blew up
and real snow inside and that you had a goat.
Kids, right? I'm not sure what he means. Do
you have any ideas?
    Lydia

I opened a third email from Olivia Larson's mom,
Jennifer, to confirm they were going to be pretty
much the same.

Hello Miss Smith,
    Olivia mentioned to me that she went
sledding during class today. She's always
had an imagination, but I can't imagine how
that's possible with no snow on the ground.

She also said there was a goat in class. She insists it was real and I'm concerned by the level of detail in her story. Do you have any thoughts about this?
Jennifer

Thought so. I opened a word document and began formulating a generic response, saying something about science lessons, combining biology and weather. I also made sure to explain the goat was a rental from a petting zoo. Suddenly, I heard a metallic thud from under the desk and jumped.

"Meh."

I had completely forgotten the goat was still here.

"Yeah, yeah. I'll let you out when I'm done."

A few minutes later, my response was perfectly crafted. It was ambiguous but had enough information to satisfy the parents...theoretically. I went back to my inbox and saw that I had 19 new messages again. Where did those three new ones come from? The first one had the subject line *Do Good for Others*. The next one below it said *Kindness. Pass it on.* The last one was something about *How it can pay to help.* I looked at the sender's email address and saw they call came from the same person. Who was candycanego_at1225@gmail.com? And why were they sending me emails about volunteer projects? I have no interest in volunteering, but somehow I must have ended up on an email distribution list. I marked those three emails as read and deleted them without opening them. I responded to all the parent emails by copying and pasting my prepared reply and began packing up to leave for the day. I grabbed my purse and went to turn out the lights when I heard a bleat from under the desk.

"Oh. Right."

I moved the sled away from the desk legs so the goat could come out. He was going to follow me anyway. I locked my classroom door on the way out and walked to the parking lot, trailed by the clicking of goat hooves. I got to my car and opened the backseat for the goat to hop in. I threw the back door shut and climbed into the driver seat. I put the key in the ignition and the car came to life.

"Deck the halls with boughs of holly..."

The goat bleated excitedly from the backseat and my phone went off. It was Mom. I stared at the phone for a few seconds and watched it ring, wondering if I should answer or not. She might want to see if I can come to a family gathering...but it might also be important. I turned the music down.

"Hello?"

"Hi, Eliza dear. How are you?"

"Good. How are you?"

"Good. Say, do you have any plans this evening?"

Yep. Thought so. "Uh, well..."

"I'm with Karen and Nancy at Karen and Frank's house. Nicole is here, too, and we thought you'd like to join us."

"I see." Where would they get that idea?

"I know you're probably busy." Even from a few miles away, Mom could still lay on the guilt.

"Yeah, I can't –" Two candy cane horns butted me softly on the arm from the back seat of the car. I looked at the goat knowingly. "Be there for about another half an hour."

Mom squealed. "They'll be so happy you're coming."

"Yeah. I'll see you soon. Bye, Mom."

I hung up and drove off. I dropped the goat at home and hoped he'd stay there long enough for me to go visit for no more than an hour. I had bought a new package of cookies on the way home last night, so that should keep him entertained for a while at least. I got to Karen and Frank's house and knocked on the door. Nancy answered.

"Oh. It's you."

I smiled and raised my eyebrows and walked past her into the living room. Frank was seated in a rocking chair, facing Mom and Karen on the couch. They were surrounded by stacks of clear plastic tubs. Nancy followed me in.

"Nice of you to join us," Nancy said curtly.

I gritted my teeth. "Yeah."

"Well, sit down." She gestured to a recliner next to the couch and she took a seat next to Mom.

"So, we just finished cleaning out Jackie's apartment." Mom indicated the tubs. "And Karen was debating if she wanted to put her things into storage or donate them."

"I can't give up *all* of her cat things. She loved them so much." Karen pulled out a white ceramic kitten with blue eyes and a pink bow around its neck and cradled it in one arm.

Nicole walked into the room, popped something into her mouth, chewed, and swallowed. She must have been back for winter break this time. I don't envy all the traveling she has done the past week.

"Hi, Eliza." She sat on the floor next to my chair.

"Hi."

"It's strange you never got Jackie a real cat when she was younger," Nancy said, pulling out a woven blanket with a picture of a cat pawing a fishbowl.

"*I* wanted to. But it just never worked out." Karen shot Frank a look and he muttered something about worthless beasts.

"At least Eliza didn't bring her goat with her again," Nancy said.

"You have a goat?" Nicole put her phone down.

"Had. It was a present for Avery…" I wondered what kind of havoc he was wreaking on my house right now. I grabbed the hem of my shirt and began to worry it.

"I hope you returned that thing," Nancy said, folding the blanket and returning it to the tub.

"Absolutely. It was just a rental."

If only.

"Wish I could have seen it," Nicole said.

"It was actually kind of cute," Mom said.

"Yeah. It was really cute when the goat ruined my skirt." Nancy snapped the lid back on the tub she set the blanket in.

"Oh, come on, Nance. It was just water," Mom said.

"Just like you put on it when you wash it," Karen added, dusting the ceramic kitten's head with her fingers.

"Yeah, Mom. Do you not wash your skirt ever? That's just gross." Nicole giggled.

I couldn't believe it. Were they defending me?

Nancy scoffed and went off to the kitchen. Karen turned to me and her face lit up. "Oh, I have something for you."

She set the ceramic kitten down and got up to go back to the bedrooms. Mom was staring contemplatively out the window and Nicole was playing on her phone again.

"When does Adam come back from Africa?" Frank asked.

"Middle of February." I had to admit, it would be

nice for my brother to be back in the States. Then they could ask him about himself and go back to fawning over Adam directly.

"Oh, yes. Your dad did say that."

"Mm-hm."

"Almost done with school?"

"Tomorrow."

"Hmm…."

Karen reappeared with a small box and handed it to me without a word. I opened the lid to reveal a beautiful set of opal earrings. October's birthstone. I looked at Karen, touched by the unexpected and kind gesture.

"They were a present for…" Karen heaved and tears began to fill her eyes. "I just miss her so much."

"I know," Mom said soothingly while Karen grabbed a tissue and blew her nose. Nicole got to her knees to look over the armrest on my chair.

"Nice." She nodded in approval. "I always liked opals. My birthstone is peridot though, so I get a lot of that. I hate green." She returned to her phone and sat down again.

"Thank you," I said.

"I hope you like them," Karen said through a sniffle. "I just figured you should have them since it's your birthstone, too."

"They're beautiful." I put on one earring.

"We thought of you a lot when we were cleaning

out Jackie's things, actually."

They did? That's surprising. I spotted a Journey t-shirt in one tub.

"You two had a lot in common. I'm not sure why you didn't hang out more," Mom said.

We didn't hang out because she sang in the school choir and she was on the quiz bowl team. She played sports, she got good grades and everyone loved her. She was popular. I'm tone deaf, was never involved in extra-curricular activities and I have no athletic talent. I was mediocre. She wouldn't want to, let alone have time to, spend with me. I kept my distance to respect that.

"Hmm," I responded.

"She always talked about how much she loved you but didn't think you'd want to spend time with her," Karen said, returning the ceramic kitten to storage.

"It's true," Nicole chimed in. "Mom, can we order pizza?"

"Pizza sounds like a great idea," Frank said.

"Sure." Nancy picked up her purse and grabbed a credit card from her wallet to give to Nicole. "Get two larges."

I was flabbergasted.

Maybe Jackie acted the way she did because of the way I acted.

My family always seemed to brush me off, but maybe they only did that because I distanced myself from them. Was this…more about me than about them?

Well, except Nancy. I think she's just a pill.

* * *

Stuffed with pizza, I arrived home later that night to find the goat waiting for me in the bedroom.

"Meh."

"Uh-huh." I pulled off my shirt and walked to my dresser, where the straw goat was still standing next to the green gift bag with the card inside. I pulled out the card and read it again, then looked at the real goat who was enjoying the suede slippers I left at the side of the bed.

I had tried giving him treats and a gift, but that hadn't worked. I hadn't received a single gift from him, either. He probably wasn't here to give me presents, especially since Jackie told me I was on the naughty list (whatever). I had also done everything I could think of to celebrate and prepare for Christmas and the goat was still here. By process of elimination, there was one option left. The card also said that in some versions of the story, the yule goat scared children. I was an elementary school teacher with easy access to kids. Maybe I had to terrify my class to get rid of the goat.

But how?

I pulled the slippers away from the goat, put them in a dresser drawer and slammed the drawer shut. I lay down and began tossing around different ideas to frighten my class...but not too much.

I'm not that heartless.

17

Chaos Erupted

At the headquarters, Present began to grab the holly crown that had fallen off his head and his hair tumbled in front of his face. He screamed when he saw that it was grey instead of the sumptuous brown it had once been.

"My beautiful hair!" Present cried as he clutched chunks of grey in his fists.

Elf was near the fireplace with Past, whose flame had shrunk to one third its original size. Elf's hands had become translucent, but he did his best to pump bellows to reignite Past's head.

"I feel so sorry for you." Past sounded like he had sucked down a whole balloon's worth of helium. The flame flowed to the side as the air from the bellows hit it.

"Krampus, can you help me over here?" Elf looked across the room to a corner where Krampus was partially hidden behind a chair. A smaller Jólaköturinn was seated next to Krampus, licking his paws.

"*Nein.*"

"Why not?"

"*Mein Umhang ist weg.*"

"Your cape is gone?" Past squeaked.

"So? You can still help."

"*Nein.*"

"Why not?" Elf was exasperated.

"*Ich bin nackt,*" Krampus replied sheepishly.

"Mew."

"Your lower half is goat legs. They're covered in fur. How could you possibly be naked?"

"How do I fix my hair?" Present asked as he surveyed the new grey color out of the corners of his eyes.

"Krampus!" Elf shouted.

"*Ich brauche meinen Umhang.*"

"You don't need your cape. Just come here."

"*Nein.*"

Elf groaned. Past's head had grown back to half its original size, but at the rate Elf was going it would still be a while before it returned to normal. Yet to Come wagged a finger at Krampus and then floated over to help Elf. His bony fingers had become hollow and the tips had disappeared, so he could now push air out the ends. He pointed at Past, took a deep breath, and a large rush of air shot out, making Past's head momentarily swell to three times its actual size.

"Whoa!" Past shook his head when it was back to normal. Elf set the bellows down.

"Now, can we do something about my hair?" As Present grabbed a chunk of it, his hand brushed his face. Noticing something different, he felt around and registered the deep wrinkles for the first time. "MY FACE!"

"Now, Present..." Elf tried his best to stay calm and be a pillar of comfort.

"It's happening. We're all disappearing!" Present screamed.

"I don't want to die," Past wailed.

"Meow!" The candle on Jólakötturinn's head had just blown out.

Yet to Come, unable to etch shapes into stone anymore, drew a tombstone and *R.I.P.* in the air.

"We're not going to disappear," Elf said, putting a hand out. "OH MY GOD!"

His hand had gone from translucent to completely transparent, and he fainted.

"Great. Now what do we do?" Present looked from Elf, unconscious on the floor, to Past.

"I don't know. Julbok has one more day and then we're going to be gone forever."

"*Wir müssen mit Julbok sprechen. Und hol mehr*

Hilfe," Krampus said from behind his chair.

"Yes, we should talk to Julbok, and get more help, but how? We can't leave in this condition," Past said.

"What?" Present had picked up Elf and was fanning him with his hand.

"Ich werde gehen."

Past studied Krampus skeptically. "You want to talk to Julbok and find more help?"

"Ja."

"And you won't drag anyone to Hell?"

"Nein."

"Okay." They were out of options. Past didn't like the idea but didn't see another way it could work. "You need a cape, though." Past tapped his lip with his index finger.

"But Krampus's cape disappeared." Present lay Elf on the table and Yet to Come started blowing a slow stream of air on his face.

Past looked at Present with a raised eyebrow. "You have a robe."

Present's eyes widened. "No."

"Come on."

"I've already lost my hair and face. Don't take my robe, too."

"Then we have nothing to do but sit and wait until we completely disappear by tomorrow. Krampus can't leave without a cape."

Present sighed. He wanted to help, but he really

loved his robe. It was so much a part of his identity, he didn't know how he could survive without it. But if he didn't give it to Krampus so he could travel, they would all just disappear, and it wouldn't matter anyway. He looked anxiously around the room, contemplating his options. Then he spotted the chair Krampus was hidden behind and looked at Past.

"Promise you won't look?"

"Yes." Past had absolutely no interest in seeing what was under Present's robes. Yet to Come used his finger to cross the spot where his heart would be.

"Okay. Here goes."

Present went to the chair. He and Krampus stood back to back as he took off his robe and handed it over. Amazingly, Krampus was only slightly smaller than Present, so the robe fit perfectly. Covered again, Krampus stepped out from behind the chair.

"Hier geh Ich."

Krampus lifted the edge of the robe, did a pivot, and he was gone. Yet to Come had floated over to the chair where Present was hiding and began to bob up and down as if laughing.

"You promised! And it's cold," Present responded indignantly and moved his hand lower.

Past rolled his eyes.

18

Wednesday, December 23rd

On Wednesday morning, I woke up feeling kind of groggy. I had a strange dream where there was a furry horned demon creature at the foot of the bed. It had long claws and a snake-like tongue and it was wearing a green robe. The goat bleated at it and it responded, but it didn't speak English. The goat bleated at it again and then I woke up and it was gone. The sheets were tattered at he foot of the bed, though, so the goat must have gotten hungry and decided to snack in the middle of the night. He was sleeping in the corner of the bedroom but woke up and greeted me before I went to work. Alone.

For the first time in five days, the goat wasn't stalking me. Weird, but I wasn't going to complain. Progress was progress.

When I got to work, I walked by Kylie's classroom

and saw a sub writing their name on the board. It was only a half day, but Kylie must have called in sick…or something happened. Something told me that I should check in with her just in case.

Hey! Hope you're feeling better.

She responded seconds later.

Thanks. I'm really going to miss her. It's gonna be so lonely without a pet in the house.

Oh, no. My heart sank. Sia was only four years old.

hug When did it happen?

Maybe not the best response, but better than "Do you want a goat?" anyway.

This morning. I'm at the vet now. She's going to be put down as soon as they come back in.

I'm so sorry.

Me, too. I need to get out and distract myself. Drinks later?

Sure. I'll pick you up after work.

Okay. See you then.

I looked at the time: 25 minutes until students were supposed to be here. I still hadn't figured out how to scare them, so I turned on the computer. Web browser opened, I tapped the keyboard thinking about what to search for and "scary Christmas" popped into my head. I typed it in and the very first result was something called the Mari Lwyd. I clicked on the page and read that people in Wales run around with a decorated horse skull and go to houses asking for drinks in exchange for a song.

Sounded like caroling to me. Scariest Christmas tradition of them all.

The next result was for Krampus. A Christmas monster who punishes the bad kids before St. Nicholas arrives. He was usually depicted with long claws and a serpentine tongue. Was Krampus the "he" Jackie warned me about? The dream I had last night.

I got chills and exited the web browser immediately. I spun around in my chair and couldn't help but notice that one of the snowmen sleds had white panels that were rounded at one end. The perfect shape for drawing on eye and nose sockets and the outline of teeth to make a quick horse skull. Using the leverage of my desk and body weight, I pried off one of the panels and grabbed a black permanent marker from my desk drawer.

I drew two ovals near the rounded edge of the panel for nostrils and two circles near the flat end for eyes. I added some contour lines near the center on each side and grabbed a piece of paper to cut out ears. I glanced up at the clock again and hastily drew black triangles for dimension on the ear shapes. I taped on the ears and cringed a little bit.

It wasn't as elaborate at the pictures of the Mari Lwyd I saw online, but I didn't have much to work with, did I? I propped it up in front of my desk just as my students started to come in.

Aubrey Moskowitz and Aiden James whispered to each other and giggled when they looked at it. Tommy Carter just looked confused.

"Miss Smith, is that supposed to be a picture of the reindeer that was here on Monday?" Olivia Larson asked, walking to her desk.

"No." I sighed.

I knew I wasn't much of an artist, but this was just depressing. The makeshift Mari Lwyd failed to have the desired effect. Defeated, I moved the panel and set it back up against the wall next to the sled it came from and inspiration hit me. Today we were going to start with science. I picked up my teacher's edition science book from the desk and turned to face the class. Time for plan B.

"Okay, everyone. Let's turn to page 40 in your science books and we'll talk about scorpions, spiders, and rattlesnakes."

My students flipped through the pages of their books excitedly and pointed animatedly at the pictures of the desert animals.

So much for scaring them.

* * *

The next few hours until noon were a blur. Right

at noon, the lunch bell rang (taking the place of the dismissal bell today) and I was out the door. Since scaring my class had failed, I instead focused on ways to cheer Kylie up and formulated the perfect plan. I could worry about getting rid of the goat later. On my way to get her I stopped at the humane society. There was only one guy behind the counter (who was wearing an elf hat, no less). He was busy with a couple who were filling out adoption papers and there was a family behind them. It would be a while, so I wandered back toward the animal area.

I went to the cats first and, as I scanned through them, I found the grey kitten that had been in the box at the back door the other day. It was curled up on a plush looking blanket in one corner of its cage. I got closer to the cage and it opened its eyes. They were green and seemed eerily familiar. It blinked at me with what seemed like recognition. I looked at the paper attached to the cage.

> *Name: Jul*
> *Gender: Female*
> *Spayed / Neutered: Yes*
> *Declawed: No*
> *Breed: American Shorthair*
> *Age: Approx. 2 months*

Look at that. She was probably also born in

October. Letting the paper fall back to the cage, I was transfixed by the eyes of the kitten. She came up to the edge of the cage and arched her back, mewing and trying to get me to pet her. I stuck my finger in and she rubbed it with her head. Something about this cat just seemed so familiar.

Mesmerized, I began to turn around and immediately bumped into a guy with long hair and a beard who must've been standing behind me. As he steadied me, his hands on my shoulder, I felt an overwhelming sense of calm. The way the light from the ceiling fell around his head almost looked like a halo. He was wearing a humane society shirt and holding a litter scooper and plastic bag.

"She just came in." He nodded toward Jul.

"Huh."

"She was left in a box on the porch out back." He opened the door to Jul's cage and started scooping dirty litter into the plastic bag. "There was a goat tied up to the handrail that day, too."

"Oh. Imagine that." I looked at the ground and shuffled my feet.

"The owners didn't fully appreciate them, I guess."

He finished scooping litter and looked at me knowingly. Was there a camera at the back door or something? Did he figure out somehow that I was the one who left the goat?

"Too bad."

"Yep." He scratched Jul between the ears, and she purred softly. Her face even looked like she was smiling. He closed the cage door and moved to the cage of an adult Maine Coon. It seemed calm and began rubbing its head against his hand as he reached in to scoop out its litter box. Even as he worked, it seemed to want his attention.

"The cats really like you."

"Yeah. One of my favorite things about animals is their unconditional love."

When he was done scooping the Maine Coon's litter box, he scratched down its back. It mewed contentedly and he closed the cage door, moving on to the cage of an orange tabby cat. It was sitting in the back corner of its cage, hissing at him when he approached.

Didn't seem very loving to me.

I watched silently as the cat recoiled when the man reached in and scooped out the litter box.

I bit my lip and hoped he wouldn't get scratched.

After a couple of scoops, he reached into his pocket and pulled out a treat. He set the treat down in the front of the cage and closed the door. Tentatively, the cat moved to the treat and ate while it watched the man. It then mewed happily and rubbed against the cage bars, trying to get the man's attention.

"Woah," I breathed. "How'd you do that? I was

sure that cat was going to scratch you a second ago."

The man turned from the cage he was working in to chuck the orange cat under the chin through the cage bars. "Nah. You just have to treat them the way you want to be treated."

"Oh."

He moved on to the next cage. "At least that's what I've always found. Be kind. Show that you appreciate them, and they'll be kind and appreciate you."

"Hmm…" This was beginning to feel very personal. I shuffled my feet.

"There are lots of animals here that need good homes." He finished in the current cage and faced me. "And there's a discounted adoption fee for the holidays. But you're not here for a pet, are you?"

"Actually, I was hoping to get a gift card."

"Of course. Come with me."

He led me to the front desk where he began to fill out a gift certificate. The man in the elf hat had disappeared and the waiting family eagerly discussed what they would name their new dog.

"How much is this going to be for?"

"How much are the adoption fees?"

"Regular, $120. $60 through December."

"$120 then, I guess." Eek! I was shocked that came out of my mouth.

There were a few pet supplies for sale in the lobby

area, so I justified it by thinking that if Kylie wanted to get a new pet before the year was over, she could pick some new toys or a friend for it. Whatever she decided. The man finished filling out the certificate, I paid, and left.

* * *

I got to Kylie's house only about a half hour later than I intended. I parked on the street and walked up to the door, certificate in hand. I rang the doorbell, and seconds later, the door opened. Kylie's eyes were red and her cheeks were tear stained.

"Hi," she said meekly.

"How are you doing?"

"I'm okay."

"Sorry I'm a little late – but I have something for you." I held up the fresh humane society gift certificate. She examined it briefly and looked up at me. "Whenever you're ready."

Jul flashed into my thoughts. I blinked to clear them. I don't need a cat right now.

"Thank you." She hugged me and smiled through fresh tears.

"Mm-hm." I knew then she'd be okay.

"Where do you want to go?" She wiped her eyes and stuck the certificate in her purse as we walked to my car.

"How about that place on 2nd Street?"

"Perfect."

It was a little after 1:30, so only a couple of other people were eating when we arrived.

"Just the two of you?" the hostess asked. She jingled as she approached the hostess stand and I noticed her large silver bell earrings.

"Yep," I said, and Kylie nodded.

"Okay." The hostess grabbed two menus and sets of silverware. "Right this way." She led us to a cozy two-person booth by a window. "Your server will be right with you."

"Thanks," Kylie said as the hostess turned to walk back to her post.

"So," I said.

"So."

"Are you hungry?"

"Not really. Still kind of shaken from this morning, honestly."

Damn it. I was starving but didn't want to be the only one eating.

"Makes sense."

"Yeah."

"Would you want to split an appetizer?"

"Sure." Kylie looked at the menu for a second. "Mozzarella sticks?"

"Works for me."

The server arrived beside the table. "Hello. I'm

John and I'll be taking care of you. Can I start you two off with something to drink?"

I looked at Kylie. She looked at me and smiled meekly. "Margarita on the rocks."

"Me, too."

"Two margaritas." John wrote it down on his pad. "And do you two need some extra time or are you ready to order?"

Three drinks and two plates of mozzarella sticks between us and a couple of hours later, Kylie was as cheered up as she was going to get. I returned her to her house and walked her to her door to say goodbye.

"Thanks again for going out. I really appreciate it."

"Anytime," I said.

"I probably won't get to the humane society before the end of the year, but I can't wait to get a new pet eventually." Kylie patted her purse where the certificate was safely tucked away.

"Good."

"Did you look at the animals while you were there? See anything good?"

"Yeah..." I thought of Jul again for the thousandth time.

Kylie smiled. "I'll have to take a look on their website before I go in person. Otherwise I might adopt them all."

"Good idea." I smiled. "Well, I should get going but I'll see you later."

"Yep. See you later." Kylie waved as she walked into her house.

I went back to my car and began driving home. Jul had been on my mind since I stopped at the humane society earlier and, when I passed the turn-off to get there, I veered over to take it.

This time when I walked in there was no line at the counter, so I walked directly up to the guy in the elf hat.

"Hello, hello!" He smiled warmly at me.

"Hi."

"What can I help you with?"

"I'm looking to adopt a cat."

"Great. Did you have one in mind? Or do you want to take a look at them?" He came out from behind the counter and we started walking toward the cat area.

"Her name is Jul."

"Ah, yes. She's a new arrival—very sweet."

"Yeah, the other guy sold me on her earlier."

"Other guy?" He stopped in front of the door to the cat area.

"Mm-hm. Long hair? Beard?"

"You were here earlier today?"

"Yeah."

"Huh. Wonder who that could have been. Usually

179

the volunteers check in with me and I thought I was supposed to be alone today."

"Oh, come on. The guy with the really long hair...and...long beard..."

And halo...

Oh my God.

19

The End

I walked up to Karen and Frank's house with Jul in a carrier in one hand and a bag of cat supplies in the other. I knocked on the door and took a deep breath as I waited. This was completely out of the blue. I'd never just show up like this let alone bring them a cat. But that same nagging feeling that told me I should go back to the humane society told me that I should bring Jul here instead of taking her home. Or to Kylie.

This is where she belongs. I just hope they accept her. Frank answered the door.

"Eliza! This is..." He looked down at the carrier and saw the cat inside. "...a surprise. Hey, Karen?"

We walked into the living room. "Sorry to just show up like this," I said.

"It's okay." Frank looked hesitantly at the cat again.

"Eliza! What…" Karen looked down at the carrier. "What's in the carrier?"

"This is Jul." I set the carrier down on the floor and proceeded to open the door. Jul tentatively took a step and looked around, sniffing the air.

"You brought us a cat?" Frank looked at me.

"Because Jackie loved them?" I tried.

"Oh, for cute!" Karen watched as Jul ran (more like leaped, actually) a lap around the room.

"Yeah, it's cute but we really don't…"

At the sound of their voices, Jul looked in our direction and immediately ran to Frank's ankles and rubbed. After a few seconds, she was rubbing Karen's ankles and purring. Karen picked her up. Jul licked her face.

"Really don't what, Frank?" Karen handed Jul to him and Jul began batting at his earlobes.

"Need a cat." Frank held Jul out so she couldn't reach his ears anymore. "It'll just scratch up the furniture."

"We can get little stoppers for her claws. Keep her nails trimmed. Get a scratching post, even."

"Okay, but we don't have any food dishes, or a litter box," Frank said, trying a second tactic. I rattled the large plastic bag full of cat supplies I had purchased. "And the litter box will stink up the house."

"We'll clean it every day." Karen scratched Jul

behind the ears as Frank continued to hold her at arm's length. "Come on. Weren't we just talking about how everything happens for a reason? Maybe this cat is supposed to be with us now."

"It'll take a while to get into the vet to get her fixed, and then there are the vaccinations…"

"The humane society took care of that already." I smiled.

"Frank," Karen said.

"What if someone comes over and they're allergic to cats?" Frank was really stretching for an argument now. He must have known he was probably going to lose this battle.

"Well, if you don't want her I'll just take her home," I offered.

Jul mewed and I could see Frank's resolve begin to waver. He brought her closer to his body. He looked into Jul's eyes and I saw recognition wash over his face. She licked his cheek and his body visibly relaxed. Jul had found her forever home.

"That's okay, Eliza. You brought her all the way here. We can keep her for a while. See how things go."

Karen's eyes lit up. "Really?"

"Yeah."

Frank handed Jul back to Karen and watched as Karen held Jul on her chest and scratched behind her ears.

"Well, I'll see you later," I said. "Enjoy."

Frank and Karen didn't even notice I'd spoken, they were so smitten with Jul. I smiled; it was the happiest they'd looked in a couple of weeks. I quietly opened the door and left.

* * *

When I got home, it seemed eerily quiet except for a fire crackling in the fireplace. Great. The goat was still here. I went through every room in the house trying to find him, but he was nowhere to be seen.

For days he was my shadow, but now I have no idea where he is. When I got to the bedroom, even the straw yule goat and bag it had come in were missing from my dresser. Odd things for a burglar to take, but okay. Must have been the Grinch. Just to be safe though, I riffled through the jewelry box where my best jewelry was (including the now complete opal earring and necklace set) and made sure my small electronics were in the usual places. Everything else seemed to be accounted for, so it really was just the goats that were gone. I briefly contemplated calling the police to report a goat-napping but decided that I'd settle instead for sleeping with a knife in the nightstand just in case whoever it was came back.

I returned to the living room and the fire illuminated the space below the miniature tree where a dull shimmer caught my eye. There was a gift wrapped in green paper. Curious, I picked it up. It was rectangular and fairly light. Where had this come from? I shook it and then tore away the paper to reveal a book. *A Christmas Carol* by Charles Dickens.

I knew instantly who had left it. Snarky goat.

I looked at the fire and returned my gaze to the book in my hand. My eyes moved again to the fire and I knew what I had to do.

I tossed the book on the couch and went to the kitchen. I opened the fridge to get out milk and grabbed the mug Kylie had given me from the cupboard. I dumped the mug's contents onto the counter, selected a packet of cocoa at random and poured the powder into the mug. I ripped the plastic wrapper off a candy cane to mix the cocoa and put the mug in the microwave to heat it up. As it spun around, I sucked the candy cane.

Twirling the candy cane in my mouth, I watched the numbers on the microwave count down and my phone suddenly felt very heavy in my back pocket.

Candy cane in one hand, I pulled out my phone and dialed my mom. She picked up after three rings.

"Hi, Mom!"

"Eliza, hi."

"Are you guys doing anything tonight for Christmas Eve?"

"Steve, Nancy and Nicole are coming over for dinner with Tim, Rachel and Avery. Frank and Karen will join us later. Why? Did something happen?"

"No." Why would she think that something happened? I really needed to call more, apparently. "I just thought I'd join you."

"Oh! That'd be wonderful, dear. Dinner's at 6."

"Okay. I'll see you then."

"I'm so glad. I'm sure Karen and Frank will be happy to see you, too. She said they have a surprise for us."

"I can't imagine what that would be." I smiled, thinking of Jul.

"Well, we'll find out tonight. See you in a few hours!"

"Yep. See you then."

I hung up the phone and returned it to my pocket just as the microwave beeped. Returning the candy cane to my mouth, I opened the microwave and pulled out the now steaming cup of cocoa.

Perfect. Now I was going to curl up on the couch and actually read this book I'd heard so much about.

Epilogue

The Christmas spirit headquarters was empty and dark. The only light came from a small fire that was clinging to life in the fireplace. A breeze came in through the windows and blew across the room. The fire suddenly exploded and with a brilliant flash, Julbok returned from Earth.

"Meh," he called. His voice echoed across the high, vaulted ceiling. No one was there to answer.

Julbok walked to the center of the room, the clicking of his hooves reverberating. He pivoted in a full circle, just to make sure he hadn't missed anything. Once he had scanned the whole space, he went to a window to see if the other spirits were waiting for him outside. Nothing. The other spirits had never hidden from him before.

"Meh!"

Growing more frantic, Julbok saw that the door was open. He ran across the room to it and peered around the corner. He didn't see anything outside but ventured through the door anyway. It was worth investigating.

As Julbok left the room, turning to the left, one of the torches on the wall slowly began to glimmer and roared to life.

The Ghost of Christmas Past emerged from the right side of the doorway and floated to the center of the room. His flame-like head was burning brighter than ever.

"It worked!" He smiled, did a happy spin and ended up facing the window, and looking through it, he could see a glowing red dot in the distance. It grew larger as the silhouette of an animal became more and more distinct.

Past knew exactly what it was.

It was a brown reindeer and it sailed gracefully through the window, galloping right up to Past upon landing. A bull with fuzzy cream-colored antlers on his head, he was wearing a black collar with a sprig of holly around his neck and his nose was like a bulb that glowed red.

The reindeer greeted Past with a snort and butted him with his antlers.

Past crossed his arms.

"Where have you been?"